THE KEY TO MURDER

Kevin O'Hagan

Grosvenor House
Publishing Limited

The right of Kevin O'Hagan to be identified as the author of this
work has been asserted in accordance with Section 78
of the Copyright, Designs and Patents Act 1988

The book cover is copyright to Kevin O'Hagan
Cover design by Tom O'Hagan

This book is published by
Grosvenor House Publishing Ltd
Link House
140 The Broadway, Tolworth, Surrey, KT6 7HT.
www.grosvenorhousepublishing.co.uk

This book is a work of fiction. Any resemblance to
people or events, past or present, is purely coincidental.

A CIP record for this book
is available from the British Library

ISBN 978-1-80381-328-8

Previous novels by the author

Battlescars
No Hiding Place
Last Stand
Killing Time
A Change of Heart
Blood Tracks

Author's Note

Some cities, towns, locations and people mentioned in this novel exist in real life. Landscapes and layouts though take on another imaginary life in this book. All the characters are purely fictional as are their stories. Thank you for indulging me to help in creating this book.

To family and friends, past and present

About the Author

Kevin lives just outside Bristol with his wife. He has three grown-up children and four grandchildren.

Since he was a child, Kevin has had a passion for writing, but has no formal writing training. Everything he has learnt has been a personal voyage of discovery.

'*If you want to get better at writing, then write.*' This is one of his favourite sayings.

The Key to Murder is his 7th work of fiction to date.

Kevin is a semi-retired, world-renowned martial artist. He holds an 8th Dan black belt in Jujutsu after 45 plus years training and teaching. These days he still teaches part time.

His hobbies include reading, writing, playing guitar, going to the gym and travelling.

www.kevinohagan.com

Acknowledgements

Thank you as always to my daughter Lauren for proofreading the manuscript and providing her advice and suggestions.

Also, big thanks to Jackie Haining Strange for a follow-up reading and valuable feedback.

My thanks also to my son Tom for another excellent book cover design.

My gratitude and thanks to all at Grosvenor House Publishing for your support and guidance throughout the publishing process.

Last but not least, big thanks and love to my wife Tina for her loyal support of my writing.

A Word from the Author

Going back some years ago, I had a dream of writing a fictional book. I am an avid reader and I always marvelled at how the writer could put together such great plots, characters and words.

I had written many articles for martial arts publications and also a handful of martial arts instructional books. I then tried my hand at some short stories, but my goal was to write that novel.

To get to the levels I had achieved in the martial arts world, I knew what hard work, discipline and dedication was about. To do the same with my writing, I was going to have to put in as much effort.

I have no formal writing experience and I didn't attend university. But what I did have was a creative imagination and dozens of stories floating around in my head.

Now I needed to learn how to get those ideas down in print.

Here we are now in 2022 and this is my seventh fictional book to date.

I really can't believe how far I have come, but I am still learning every day.

I still stand on the shoulder of giants.

Amongst my favourite authors are James Patterson, Michael Connelly and Peter James. Masters of their craft. Every time I read one of their books, I learn something new about writing. These guys, and their like, inspire me to write better.

I can't measure my success in monetary gain because making a living from writing is a hugely competitive arena, but what I do have is a deep sense of satisfaction when I take an idea and follow it through to its fruition in the form of a book.

If people read it and enjoy it, then there is no better feeling for a writer and author.

So, follow your dreams and never give up on what you want to achieve in life.

If you want it bad enough, you will succeed.

I hope you enjoy *The Key to Murder.*

Kevin O'Hagan
August 2022

Prologue

Joseph Caine alighted the train at Bristol Temple Meads Railway Station at platform one. He checked around for any fellow passengers that may look like they were following him. Caine couldn't sniff any Old Bill. He sensed that he was okay and had arrived here without any unwanted company.

He studied the signs around the busy platform for the exit and tightly gripped the black holdall he held in his right hand.

He would be glad to offload it.

To make sure that he wasn't under surveillance, he had chosen to use public transport in the way of a taxi to catch a tube and, finally, the train that had brought him to his destination from London.

He now headed towards the turnstile gates.

The place was busy on this Friday afternoon.

Lots of commuters heading for home after a hectic week.

Bristol Temple Meads was a magnificent structure, built in 1839 for the Great Western Railway by the legendary engineer Isambard Kingdom Brunel.

The grandeur of the building was lost on Caine as he hurriedly exited the turnstiles after scanning a QR code from his phone.

He looked behind him again.

Passengers walked along purposefully looking for their platform or stood studying the electronic boards for train times. Nobody seemed interested in him.

Mind you, Joseph Caine worked hard at being the grey man.

He didn't want to stand out in the crowd.

Going about his business undetected was of paramount importance.

The journey down from London had been a fraught one initially. Caine had been sure that he was being tailed from his home to the tube station at the Elephant and Castle on the Bakerloo line to Waterloo station. Although he had chosen three different modes of transport, he had still been nervous until he got on the train.

He had waited until the very last moment to board the 2.30pm train to Bristol and was sure that he had shaken off any potential tail. But ever the professional, he couldn't allow himself to drop his guard until he had completed his task.

Just beyond the exit barrier, he saw the shop he needed. *News Plus.*

Inside the shop at the rear was a baggage storing service called *Luggage Safe.*

He had booked his bag in online and paid for storage under the false name of Walter White on a fake credit card.

Walter White was the main character in one of Caine's favourite TV dramas, *Breaking Bad.* The actor who played him, Bryan Cranston, had done a brilliant job of portraying science teacher turned crystal meth cook to drugs baron.

Caine had enjoyed the little private joke of using the name.

Once the bag was registered, he was emailed a security tag with his name and a unique code number, which he printed and thread through his luggage's zipper.

When the bag was deposited, he would receive a receipt with the code on and also a key. On return to pick up the bag again, all he had to do was produce the receipt and key and a member of staff would retrieve it from a secure personalised locker, no questions asked.

Whatever the client decided to store was their own business and never questioned by the staff. As long as you had the key and receipt when you returned to pick up your baggage, all was good.

Perfect.

Most railway stations no longer had luggage storage due to the threat of terrorist bombings stemming back to the threat of the IRA in the 1980s and then 9/11. So, these modern storage hubs were springing up everywhere.

Luggage Safe was well known for its discreteness and client privacy. In fact, they prided themselves over it in contrast to their rivals.

You only paid for the length of time you wished to store your baggage.

Usually, it was around eight pounds a day.

People visiting a city found it an ideal way of shedding any heavy bags or cases while they were sightseeing or on business.

Before depositing the holdall he was carrying, Joseph Caine checked around one last time.

All seemed good.

He entered the shop and walked past racks of newspapers and magazines and shelves lined with every type of snack under the sun.

His stomach rumbled, a reminder he hadn't eaten since breakfast time.

He earmarked a Snickers bar to pick up after he got rid of the bag.

Moving to the rear, he found *Luggage Safe*.

He was cheerfully greeted at a large reception desk by a young woman whose name tag on her smart red blazer read Emily under the *Luggage Safe* logo.

He handed over his bag.

She checked the tag and gave Caine a receipt.

She disappeared with the bag and returned a few moments later with a key on a red fob. It had the number 79 on it.

She informed him to bring both receipt and key back with him when collecting his belongings.

Caine thanked her, took the key and put it into his inside jacket pocket along with the receipt.

He had booked the bag in for 72 hours. More than enough time just in case there were any hiccups with the person arriving to retrieve it.

Joseph Caine only trusted a person once.

He exited the shop, wolfing down his chocolate bar in three bites and headed back over to the station's washrooms.

Once inside, he scanned the area.

The place was empty, except for one cubicle door which was closed and occupied.

Caine noted this.

He ran the cold tap and splashed the cool water on his face. It felt good. He had been sweating from the long trip.

The responsibility of the bag drop had been huge.

The contents of it had been owed to a powerful and dangerous man.

Not the sort of person you would want to get on the wrong side of.

The contents were given to Joseph by his boss, another powerful and dangerous man.

A serious business transaction between two likeminded individuals.

He now gulped down a couple of handfuls of water to wet his parched throat. Looking up in the mirror, he straightened his tie and ran his fingers through his hair.

Everything was good.

The swop would be made tomorrow, and all would be sweet. He was glad to have got the holdall stashed away safely for now.

Spending the night in Bristol would now be more pleasurable without the worry of the bag and its contents. He hadn't let it out of his sight since London. It was a relief now to have his hands free.

A flush sounded and the cubicle door opened.

A big guy walked out.

He had the face of a man who had been in a few scraps in his time. He sported cauliflower ears and a broken nose.

He looked in Caine's direction.

Was he a threat? Had Caine been followed after all?

Caine's heart thumped in his chest as the man walked slowly in his direction. Discreetly reaching in a pocket of his leather jacket, he closed his hand around the small push dagger.

There was nobody else in the toilets but the pair of them.

Caine was ready to use the blade if necessary.

He held his breath as the man got closer.

Caine palmed the razor-sharp dagger.

One stab into the carotid artery and vagus nerve would take this big bastard out.

He would be dead in minutes.

Caine was poised and ready. He had done this type of thing before. That was why his boss employed him.

The man suddenly nodded in his direction and went to one of the sinks to wash his hands.

Caine breathed a sigh of relief.

False alarm.

He left the washrooms and exited the station through the main entrance, getting straight into a taxi.

"Bristol Marriott Hotel. City centre, please," he told the driver.

The car pulled away into the traffic and soon left the station behind.

Caine sat back and checked his inside jacket pocket. The key and receipt were safely there. He had covered his tracks well and outwitted the law for now.

Half the job was complete and tomorrow he would meet his contact and do the deal. All being well, he would be finished and back in London early afternoon.

He pulled out the burner phone from his pocket and texted the number he had in the directory:

Bag dropped in safe place. Will meet your man 12.00pm tomorrow as arranged.

He waited and looked at the screen. Minutes later, a text was returned:

That's good. All arranged for meet.

Joseph Caine pocketed the phone and then produced his private mobile. He searched for a number and pressed it. A moment later, a female voice answered hello.

Caine spoke.

"Karen, I'm in Bristol overnight at the usual place. Come on over for a little fun."

"Sure thing, honey. Shall I bring my little bag of tricks with me?"

"Oh yes, I look forward to it. See you at 8.00pm in the bar."

Caine smiled and disconnected the phone. Business and pleasure sometimes had to be mixed, especially with a girl like Karen.

Well, in her case, it was more pain and pleasure.

He looked out of the window and smiled to himself as the city flashed by. It had just started to rain, but it wouldn't stop play for Caine.

Chapter 1

Ronnie Moon put his mobile phone down onto the bathroom mat, took a sip of Dom Pérignon and carefully placed the Waterford crystal glass champagne flute back on the edge of the bath.

He sunk down to his neck in the bubbly water and turned on the gold-plated hot water tap with his outstretched right big toe. The water needed a little boost to keep it at the temperature he liked.

A smile of satisfaction crossed his face after receiving the call.

He now relaxed and soaked his aching muscles.

Eddie, his personal trainer, had just taken him through a tortuous one-hour gym workout, ending with half a dozen three-minute rounds on the focus pads.

He had done okay according to Eddie, who was never forthcoming with praise very often.

Eddie Sweeney was a tough customer, ex PTI in the prison service and former Scots Guard. Glaswegian, hard as granite and as fit as a butcher's dog.

If he said you had done okay, then you must have.

Ronnie contemplated this. Not bad for a 52-year-old. Especially after the shooting.

Three bullets had been removed from his body some two years ago after an attempt on his life. He should have died, but by a stroke of fate, he hadn't.

The bullets hadn't penetrated any vital organs and the shooter had made a mistake of using only a .22 calibre gun.

Fucking amateur.

Ronnie had lived to fight another day.

More lives than a cat.

The shooter didn't fare so well though.

His body was found a couple of weeks after the incident in the river Thames, minus his head and hands.

The police didn't know it was the shooter. They didn't have a clue who it was, but Ronnie did.

Some fucking muppet.

Little Russian bastard.

Part of a team who thought they could come over here and muscle in on Ronnie's London patch.

Nobody fucks with Ronnie Moon or his little empire and lives to tell the tale.

'Old school' still ruled as far as Ronnie was concerned.

* * *

The bathroom door opened and in walked Ronnie's wife, Josie.

A vivacious 35-year-old blonde.

They had been married for six years.

People had said behind Ronnie's back that he was punching well above his weight and the marriage would never last. Well, what did they know?

They were soulmates.

Third time lucky, I suppose.

His first wife, Julie, had been a lovely kid. But they married too young. School sweethearts doomed for failure.

The second one, Mandy, had been a controlling, nasty bitch. Mouth like a sewer and a tongue so sharp it could cut you.

Ronnie didn't realise all this until she began to hit the gin bottle hard after two miscarriages.

She had been like a Jekyll and Hyde character.

Josie, though, was an angel. In no way demanding and accepted him for what he was.

"Mind if I join you?" asked Josie

Ronnie grinned.

"Be my guest," he replied.

He watched her undo the white towelling robe that she was wearing and let it drop to the floor. Ronnie's eyes roamed hungrily over her toned naked body. She was a real babe and a lioness in bed.

He felt a stirring in his loins as she got into the bath and faced him stretching out her long legs and placing two ruby red nail-polished feet onto his chest.

"Glass of champagne?" asked Ronnie.

"Don't mind if I do."

Josie flashed him her gorgeous smile.

Ronnie poured a glass.

"Eddie put you through it as well?" he asked.

"Not half! Forty-minutes of circuit training. That man is an animal."

"He certainly is, my sweet, and he knows how to keep that gorgeous body of yours in shape."

Josie pinned her blonde locks up with a couple of hair clips.

"I think he fancies me."

Ronnie stopped in mid pour.

"Oh yeah? Is that right? Well, I can't blame him for that, I suppose. As long as he keeps his hands to himself. He has, I take it?"

"Of course he has," answered Josie.

Ronnie handed her the champagne, making her reach for it so her breasts were exposed out of the water. What magnificent breasts they were too.

Well, they should be. They had cost him eight grand. Worth every penny though.

Josie took the offered drink.

"Are we going out for dinner tonight or shall I phone Claude and ask him to cook here?"

"I don't mind, sweetheart. Whatever you want. I'm easy."

Josie sipped her champagne.

"I'll call Claude and get him to cook a couple of his special fillet steaks."

"Terrific," replied Ronnie.

He lay back and closed his eyes.

"A nice bottle of burgundy would go down a treat with that and then a good film after. I'll pop down to the wine cellar in a while and choose one. A pinot noir, I think."

Josie leant forward.

"Lovely, but no rush."

As she said this, her hand closed over Ronnie's penis.

He opened his eyes and grinned.

"You naughty girl. Are you trying to take advantage of me?"

Josie returned the smile.

"Yes."

"Obviously Eddie didn't quite deplete all your stores of energy."

Just then, Ronnie's mobile phone sounded. He reached for it.

"Let it ring," said Josie.

He checked the caller ID.

"Sorry, babe. I've got to take this. It's Tommy. I won't be long."

Josie huffed and let go of him.

"You and your bloody work."

Ronnie smiled, blew her an air kiss and answered the call.

Tommy Scott was Ronnie's brother-in-law. He lived in Bristol some fifty miles from Ronnie's Cotswold home. Thirty something and couldn't keep a job longer than a few weeks because he liked the booze too much and also had a penchant for recreational drugs. Not the sharpest tool in the box, but he treated Sharon, Ronnie's younger sister, like a queen.

Sharon had asked Ronnie to find a job for Tommy within the firm a few months back. At first, Ronnie wasn't sure, but he loved his younger sister unconditionally, so he found a position for her husband.

Tommy was keen, just like an excited pup. Eager to please. But Eddie had reservations due to the fact he was prone to the odd fuckup as a result of his habits. When he was on it, he could prove a liability, but recently, Ronnie had kept him in check and sober and clean.

In the business he was in, he needed loyal and trusted people around him. Tommy may have lacked experience, but being family, he had those two characteristics in spades.

So, Ronnie decided to use him for the important little jobs when he needed complete and utter confidentiality.

Also, he had heard a whisper that the Old Bill had been sniffing around some of his contacts up in London. So, he had decided not to use any of the well-known faces in his firm so as not to attract any attention to himself.

Tommy would be non-descript. A person of no interest, which was exactly what was needed on this job. Plus, it was on Tommy's doorstep in his home city of Bristol. Just far enough away from Ronnie if the heat went down.

Tommy Scott was also, unfortunately, dispensable if need be.

* * *

"Tommy, how is it? Sharon alright?"

"All good, Ronnie. She told me to give you a bell. You have another job for me?"

"Yeah. Listen, Tommy. I do have an important job for you in good old Bristol. Drive up to the house for 9.00am tomorrow and have some breakfast and I will explain all to you then rather than talking on the phone."

"Sure thing, Ronnie," replied Tommy.

"Oh, and by the way, Tommy, make sure you stay off the blow and scotch. And take a shower in the morning, have a shave and put on a bloody suit. Wear the blue one I bought you. The job is an important one and I don't want any fuckups. Got it? Right, see you 9.00am sharp and don't be late."

Before Tommy could reply, Ronnie hung up the call and looked over at Josie.

"See, I told you I wouldn't be long. Now where were we?"

* * *

Ronnie made his way down into the state-of-the-art wine cellar. He loved it down here. In fact, he loved the whole house, which he had custom built from scratch.

It was certainly something special. Even that geezer on the television that presents *Grand Designs* had been along to see it and wanted it featured on the show, but Ronnie wouldn't hear of it.

This was his bolthole and safe place.

Fuck anybody he didn't know finding out about it.

The house was a huge glass and wood affair on three levels.

The design somewhat made it resemble an old sailing galleon.

It had cost two million pounds to build, and it was situated right in the heart of the beautiful Cotswolds near the picturesque little town of Stonebridge.

This area was very exclusive, and you needed money and lots of it to live here.

That was no problem for Ronnie Moon.

Ex-London butcher at the legendary Smithfield's Market to big-time entrepreneur.

He made his millions on the surface as a very successful property developer, but behind the squeaky-clean façade, he was one of the UK's biggest arms dealers.

Not that anybody outside his close circle knew this fact.

Around here near Stonebridge, he was held in high esteem. Valuable businessman, important member of the local community and charity fundraiser.

When he was up in his birthplace of London, he would have dinner now and again with the mayor and he had a private box at his beloved West Ham United. Hammers born and bred.

Bobby Moore and Geoff Hurst were football gods to him when he watched them back in the day at the then iconic Upton Park.

He often joked that when he was shot, he bled claret and blue.

Every year he would hire out the land around his house free of charge for the annual gymkhana and Ironbridge summer fair.

He also invited the local gentry to shoot on his land. Ronnie would join them. He was a crack shot with a shotgun.

He had confessed to Josie once that he had to remind himself not to bring the 'sawn-off' one down to the shoot.

He also donated the town's centrepiece Christmas tree two years on the trot and was guest of honour to officially switch on the town lights voted above TV personality and Cotswold farmer Jeremy Clarkson.

Ronnie did admit that he was smug about that fact because he didn't like the man.

Who Wants to Be a Millionaire. Bollocks. Ronnie already was one and then some.

The people of Stonebridge loved this generous and charismatic man who had been living in the area the past three years.

In the main, he kept his two lives separate. When it came to the business of arms, he made sure nothing was done on his doorstep. Ronnie went back to London for that.

He ran a tight ship and not many people would try and take him on.

The shooting had been a result of a Russian firm trying to muscle in on some of his territory in London, seemingly suggesting to Ronnie that arms dealing here in the UK was their business and he was encroaching on it.

That had been their first mistake, cheeky bastards.

Not killing him when they had the chance was their second mistake and a costly one. The body floating in the Thames had been a statement of intent from Ronnie not to fuck with him.

Others in the past had also made that mistake.

The foundations of a past property venture near Epping Forest hid another half a dozen bodies that nobody would ever find. Yet more people who had made the costly mistake of crossing Ronnie Moon.

In relation to his shooting, Ronnie had concocted the story for the locals that he had disturbed a burglary in his London residence and was shot when he came across the thief.

This added more kudos to his reputation.

The Russian threat for now seemingly had gone away. Crawled back to Moscow with their tails between their legs, no doubt. They were probably now fighting for Putin on the front line against Ukraine. God help them though if they returned.

At this moment in time, his business empire was booming and trouble-free. Just the way he liked it.

He found the bottle of wine that he wanted and returned upstairs to the huge, bright and airy kitchen. A stainless steel and black granite worktops affair with a gleaming white island in its centre, the size of a snooker table.

The meal cooking of steak, garlic and herbs instantly hit his nostrils.

Claude Henry was a French Michelin star chef who came in when required to cook for Ronnie. He was a magician of conjuring up mouth-watering foods. He wasn't cheap, but with so many things in life, if you wanted the best, you had to pay for it. And fortunately for Ronnie Moon, he could afford it.

Making money had been a passion of his since he was a kid. He would sing in the local pubs for pocket money or deliver fruit and veg on his bike to elderly people in his place of birth East London.

Later in life, as his tastes got more extravagant, how he made his money didn't matter to him.

When you had the Cotswold home, a London flat in Knightsbridge and a villa in Marbella to run, you weren't fussy where the money came from.

With a Porsche, Ferrari, Mercedes and a Land Rover Discovery in his garage, these beauties didn't run on fresh air, not to mention the expense of his forty-foot yacht to moor.

His trusted team of accountants and lawyers knew how to juggle his finances and his books to make him look squeaky clean.

His legitimate businesses helped launder the illegal money.

The arms business was all about supply and demand and there was always some banana republic or terrorist cell who wanted them.

The revolutionaries demanded it and Ronnie supplied.

His contacts around the world were second to none. They had an inexhaustible supply of would-be anarchists, always eager to do business.

His clientele was A list.

Ronald Winston Moon was a smart cookie.

He kept his nefarious business interests well concealed.

It was all about discipline and self-control.

He had no problem with that.

His grandfather, William, had been in the Royal Marines and had instilled these attributes in Ronnie from an early age.

Ronnie's father, Michael, spent most of his time in prison, so he wasn't there with too much fatherly advice, apart from, "If you follow in my footsteps, son, don't get caught."

It was probably the only bit of advice his father ever gave him because he still remembered it and adhered to it religiously. Prison was for mugs.

* * *

Ronnie uncorked the wine and poured two generous measures into two large, long-stemmed glasses and brought them through to the living room where a huge sixty-inch television on the wall was playing *The Chase*. He was a big fan of the show and also the host Bradley Walsh.

Josie was curled up on a gigantic sofa that dwarfed her. Next to her sleeping was their German Shepherd, Harley. He lazily opened one eye as Ronnie approached the sofa and his nostrils twitched at the smell of the fillet steak cooking.

Josie accepted the wine offered and Ronnie sat down next to her. They clinked their glasses together

"Cheers," they said simultaneously.

"Claude reckons it will be about thirty minutes until he plates up," said Josie.

"Great," replied Ronnie, "I've starving."

"Must have been all that exercise," exclaimed Josie.

Ronnie smiled.

"Yeah, and I don't mean the exercise in the gym. You'll be the death of me, girl. I tell you."

Josie leant in and kissed Ronnie on the lips.

He could smell her Chanel perfume and taste the red wine on her mouth.

"Did I ever tell you I love you, Mr Moon."

"Not often enough, Mrs Moon."

They kissed again.

They turned their attention back to the television screen.

"Right, who is the chaser going to be? I say it will be the Beast," said Ronnie.

Josie shook her head.

"The Vixen. Definitely."

Ronnie laughed and pulled her to him and once again found her lips. As they kissed passionately, it was the Dark Destroyer who walked out as the chaser. For the moment, the show was forgotten.

* * *

The meal had been excellent and, as always, Claude had excelled himself.

Now Ronnie and Josie sat back alone on the sofa on their second bottle of wine watching the classic old black and white film *Casablanca*.

Ronnie's eyes were getting heavy, and Josie was coming and going with sleep.

It was late.

Turning the television off with the remote, Ronnie got up from the sofa, which woke Josie.

"Time for bed, sweetie. Go on up and I'll lock up and be straight up myself."

Josie nodded sleepily and made for the ornate glass and iron spiral staircase in the corner of the room, which would bring her upstairs.

On the way up, she mused which one of the four bathrooms she would use tonight to brush her teeth in.

Ronnie carried the empty wine bottle and two glasses out into the kitchen. He put the glasses in the dishwasher and then opened up the patio doors to put the bottle out in the recycling. As he did this, the security lights came on and he heard a scuttling noise from the bushes out in the gardens.

Harley went running out of the door barking loudly.

Slightly startled, Ronnie's gaze followed the dog.

Since the shooting, he had got a little twitchy, especially at night.

He had a top-class security system fitted in the house, but the memory of him pulling up onto the drive of his London residence and getting out of his car to come face to face with a masked man aiming a Walther PP at him still sent chills down his spine.

Having said that, he was against living in a fortress here in the Cotswolds. He wanted his homelife to be as normal as possible, but also not to draw too much unwanted attention. That is why he kept the security to a minimum.

His unease suddenly dispersed as he saw a fox scurry away and climb over the wall before Harley could get to it.

"Come on, boy. Back in now," called Ronnie.

Once back inside, he felt more relaxed.

He locked the doors before drawing the blinds.

Too much bloody wine. That's what it is. Got me imagining all kind of things. This is Stonebridge in the sleepy Cotswolds, not the capital. Hardly a hotbed of crime.

He checked around downstairs, switching off lights and locking the front door, before arming the alarm system to the house.

He headed wearily up the stairs.

* * *

In the garden, a man stealthy crept from the undergrowth and scaled over the same wall that the fox had a moment or two ago. He made his way to a car parked down a dark country lane some distance from the house.

Once inside, he pulled out a mobile phone and dialled a number.

When answered at the other end, the man said in a thick Russian accent, "I am ninety-nine percent sure I have found him. I only had a fleeting glimpse, but I am sure it is Ronnie Moon. Our sources were correct."

The man hung up the call. He started up the car and disappeared into the night.

He planned to return soon and avenge the death of his younger brother Pavel.

Chapter 2

Tommy Scott stood in front of the bedroom mirror and studied his appearance. He was showered and shaved and wearing his best navy-blue suit.

He had scrubbed up alright.

Some people said he passed more than a fleeting resemblance to rock star Kelly Jones, frontman of the Welsh band, the Stereophonics.

Being off the booze and drugs for nearly six weeks had improved his skin and his eyes had a sparkle back in them that he had forgotten about.

He ran his hands through his short brown hair and then put on his wristwatch.

His wife, Sharon, sat up in bed sipping a coffee and regarded her husband.

"Very smart, love. You look the part. Handsome as well. Now I remember why I married you."

Tommy turned and faced her.

Even without her make-up on and her hair tousled from sleep, she was as pretty as a picture. She belied her 42 years.

"Well, you didn't marry me for my money. That's a cert."

Sharon brushed a few strands of her auburn hair from her face and smiled.

"You do this spot of business today for our Ronnie and you will be quids in. There might even be a permanent position for you in the firm if you keep sober and clean."

Tommy Scott felt a knot of apprehension in his stomach. He was grateful of the job Ronnie had given him, but he was nervous that he would fuck it up.

Married or not to his sister, Ronnie Moon could be a scary fucker. Tommy didn't want to let him down or get on the wrong side of him. That was for sure.

This was a fresh start for him.

His boozing and drugs antics had cost him more jobs than he could recall and had put extreme pressure on Sharon to be the breadwinner in her job as a nurse.

He had wasted copious amounts of money on his habits until he was down to begging, borrowing and stealing to feed his appetites.

When Ronnie had given him the job, he was well aware that Sharon had twisted her older brother's arm to offer it to him. Also, he knew that Sharon didn't want to live off Ronnie's charity or spend his dirty money.

She lived her life well clear of his shady dealings and had resisted all his offers of financial help. But desperate measures made her go to him this time before her husband killed himself with substance abuse.

He owed it to her to do the job right.

He knew Ronnie had as much regard for him as a dog's turd.

Tommy had met Ronnie to talk about a job vacancy in the firm and Ronnie had spelt it out plainly that he was doing Sharon a favour and thought that he was a waste of space. But he was willing to give him a trial and see if Tommy could prove him wrong.

If he fucked up, regardless of the fact that he was married to his sister, Ronnie said he would punish him before cutting him loose for good.

Tommy didn't like the sound of this, and it had given him the incentive he needed to go on the wagon.

"Do you know anything about this job then?" Tommy asked Sharon.

Sharon swallowed a mouthful of coffee.

"No. Ronnie wouldn't divulge any of his business interests and I don't want to know."

"That's what worries me," replied Tommy.

"Come here, you big baby."

Sharon opened her arms towards him.

They hugged and kissed each other.

"You are going to be fine. Now go and do it and ring me later," she said.

Tommy nodded.

Sharon was an absolute rock. He didn't deserve her.

He couldn't understand why she was still with him after all his fuckups and the blazing rows they had over the years. Yet there she was, championing his corner yet again.

* * *

Tommy went downstairs and grabbed his car keys from a dish on a side table by the front door. He opened the door and stepped out onto the porch.

It was beginning to rain. The grey skies of Bristol looked foreboding.

He couldn't afford to get his suit wet, so he nipped back inside and grabbed an overcoat off the hall stand nearly tripping over a couple of black binliners that

Sharon had stuffed with clothes for the local charity shop lying on the floor.

He slipped the coat on.

It wasn't exactly the height of fashion and he had owned it for years, but it would do.

He left the house.

Fifteen minutes later, he was heading out of the city centre in his car and following the signs for the Cotswolds and the town of Stonebridge.

Allowing for traffic, he should be there in around an hour.

* * *

Ronnie saw the grey Toyota Corolla pull into the large circular gravel drive. He had opened the main gates further down the approach road when Tommy had spoken into the wall-mounted intercom.

He watched Tommy get out of the car and head for the front door. Ronnie was impressed that he looked very sharp in his suit.

This was a good start.

For now, the rain had stopped, although the forecast was showers all day.

This was only the third time Tommy had visited the house. He was in awe of it.

Was he jealous of this place compared to his two-bedroom semi back in Bristol? You bet he was.

Ronnie was always begging Sharon to let him buy her a nice waterside flat or a stylish bungalow, but she said she would not accept his charity and that they were fine where they were.

He admired her resolve and integrity.

Tommy, on the other hand, would have bitten his hand off. He didn't share his wife's principles and ethics.

He had been a ducker and a diver all his life. Did some prison time in his younger years for receiving stolen goods and a bit of burglary. He worked on the markets for years and was always up to a bit of skulduggery. Nothing heavy, but he liked to make a few bob legally or otherwise. He had dealt with more things that had dropped off the back of a lorry than he had hot dinners.

When he met Sharon Moon on holiday in Mallorca, things changed. He fell in love immediately with this pretty, funny and happy-go-lucky girl. In a whirlwind romance, they were married in six months. That was ten years ago.

He had tried to clean up his act and hold down an honest job, but his passion for drinking, drugs and associating with some dodgy characters on a regular basis always found him letting Sharon down.

He tried the AA for his drink problem, but he might as well have gone to the breakdown service for all it did. Three of the lads he met there all became his regular drinking buddies, would you believe?

It was something that was in the family DNA. Father and grandfather alike. Two useless pissheads.

Thank fuck for his old mum, Judith, God rest her soul, for looking after him in his childhood and teenage years.

Tommy knew the reputation of the family he had married into and although at the time Ronnie had been living in Spain, his reach went far and wide. He had a visit from a couple of his heavies informing him that if he fucked up and hurt Sharon, Ronnie would be flying home to pay him a visit.

Tommy got the message and tried to toe the line, but struggled.

Ronnie had not been keen on the marriage and was very protective of his sister.

Better the devil you know, I suppose.

Sharon was Ronnie's only sibling.

They had a brother, Tony, who tragically died in a motorbike accident when he was only eighteen. The loss brought Ronnie and Sharon even closer and Ronnie being the eldest always looked out for his sister, even though she went her own way and didn't want any of her brother's riches.

For all Ronnie's wealth, Sharon refused to exploit or use it. She preferred to live her own life and not live off her brother's ill-gotten gains.

She didn't know exactly what Ronnie's other business interests were, but she knew they were heavy and the less involvement she had with her brother, the better.

It had always been a bone of contention between them in their adult lives.

So, Tommy and Sharon lived a modest existence.

Whenever Ronnie rang his sister for a catch-up, she would lie and tell him that Tommy was off the booze and holding down a job. This was easy to get away with while Ronnie was in Spain, but when he married Josie and decided to come back to the UK to live, matters were different. They could no longer pull the wool over his eyes.

The one saving grace for Tommy was that he truly loved Sharon and, even when drinking, he never harmed a hair on her head.

Ronnie had begrudgingly respected him for that and, in the end, relented to the only thing Sharon had ever asked him for and gave her husband the trial job.

God help him.

* * *

"Come on in, Tommy. You are looking sharp, my man."

Ronnie ushered the younger man through the front door.

"Go straight through to the kitchen. Fancy a bacon sarnie?"

"Yeah, that would be great. I didn't have any breakfast this morning," replied Tommy looking around him, still mesmerised by the splendour of his surroundings.

In the kitchen, Ronnie busied himself cooking the bacon. On the quiet, he fancied himself as a bit of a Gordon Ramsey.

"Help yourself to coffee, Tommy. It's just here."

Tommy grabbed a cup and poured himself one from the cafetiere on the worktop.

"Do you want one?" he asked Ronnie.

"No, better not. I've had two this morning and Josie is always on my case about cutting down on the old caffeine."

Ronnie gestured to the stools around the island.

"Park your ass down. Bacon is nearly done. So, my little sister is okay?"

"Yeah, she's all good, Ronnie."

"Still at the hospital working, I take it?"

Tommy took a sip of his coffee. It tasted great. So different from the cheap granules he was used to at home.

"You know what she's like, Ronnie. It's more of a vocation to her than a job."

"I hope you're helping out at home while she's grafting like a trojan."

Tommy felt a pang of anger inside.

"Yes, of course I am."

"Staying off the gear and booze as well?"

Tommy took another sip of coffee.

"Yes, I told you I have."

"Good," replied Ronnie.

He placed a doorstep bacon sandwich down in front of Tommy.

"Go on. Get that down your neck. Better take that jacket off and stick this tea towel in your shirt. You don't want to show up at this meet with bacon fat on your tie."

Tommy laughed nervously and did as instructed.

"So, what is this job exactly?"

Tommy watched Ronnie fill a cup with coffee, his earlier pledge on cutting down on caffeine seemingly now forgotten.

He sat down on a stool next to Tommy. His sharp emerald green eyes bored straight into him.

"Right, this is the deal."

Tommy suddenly felt his appetite fade.

"I have some serious money owed to me from an arms deal. Covid-19 and all that lockdown bollocks last year put paid to it being delivered, but now things have eased up, the money can move finally. I had a whisper from the money man that the police had been sniffing around and watching him and his operation. So, instead of just getting in a car and arranging a meeting place, the courier came by train to Bristol to put the Old Bill off the scent.

He has already deposited the money in a luggage storage shop so that he is not carrying it around in case he gets lifted. Your job is to meet him where he will give you a key and receipt to retrieve the money bag and then you bring it back here to me."

Tommy licked his lips. They were dry.

"How much money are we talking about here, Ronnie?"

Ronnie smiled.

"That's not really your concern, but so you know the importance of the job, I will tell you."

Just then, they were interrupted by Josie coming into the kitchen.

She had been out running.

Tommy's eyes couldn't help appraising her curvy body clad in a tight pink sports top, which her nipples poked through, and the clinging black leggings.

Her skin was glowing with a light sheen of sweat.

"Hello, Tommy. How's it going? Sharon all good?"

"All good thanks, Josie. You alright?"

Josie opened the fridge, looking for some orange juice.

As she did, a stray lemon fell out onto the kitchen floor.

Josie bent over to pick it up and Tommy nearly choked on his coffee as he got a magnificent view of her shapely rear.

"You alright, Tommy?" asked Ronnie.

Tommy coughed.

"Yeah, fine. Just went down the wrong way."

Josie poured her juice and picked up the glass.

"Oh well, I will leave you boys to it. I am off to grab a shower."

Tommy couldn't even let himself think about that scenario.

Christ, that was one sexy woman.

He tried to focus on the job at hand.

"Anyway, where were we? Oh yes. There is £350,000 in the bag and I want it all back safely. Understand?" continued Ronnie.

Tommy nodded, trying to stay cool.

£350,000. WTF!

"No disrespect, Ronnie, but with that amount of money at stake, wouldn't it be better if you sent one of your top boys rather than me?'

"Well, the problem with that, Tommy boy, is if the police are sniffing, they will clock them. But you are not known to the Old Bill, so you can walk around in the open unchallenged. You understand?"

Tommy nodded.

"No worries, Ronnie. It'll be safe with me. I'll have it back in no time."

"Right. The man you have to see is a geezer called Joseph Caine. I've sent a photo image of him to your phone. He is staying at the City Centre Marriott Hotel in Bristol. This is his mobile number.

He'll meet you in the hotel bar at noon today and give you what you need. Once the business is done, delete his number and photo. Nothing must be traced back to me. This Caine geezer will tell you exactly where the bag is stored, you pick it up and..."

Tommy cut in.

"And bring it back here."

"Yes, but not right away."

Tommy looked confused.

"How come?"

Ronnie took a sip of coffee, pulled a face and spooned some more sugar into it.

"I have got to go with Josie tomorrow morning to visit her old mum in the nursing home over in Brighton. It's her 75th birthday. The old girl is getting over another stroke. Probably won't even know who we are, but Josie needs to do it and wants my support. So, you look after the bag and bring it up here first thing Wednesday morning. Can you do that?"

"I'm not sure about hanging onto that money for that length of time, Ronnie. That is a big responsibility, which makes me nervous."

Ronnie put a strong arm around the younger man's shoulder and hugged it tightly. Tommy felt the man's strength.

"It's unfortunate, but I don't trust anybody else in the firm looking after the bag while I'm gone. That's why I choose you. You're ideal and I know you won't let me down or screw me over, will you?"

"No, Ronnie. Honest," replied Tommy, hoping that this would ease his brother-in-law's grip on him.

It did.

"Get the bag. Don't hang around Bristol city centre. Get straight home with it. Put it in the wardrobe and shut the door on it and forget about it until Wednesday. It'll be cool," said Ronnie.

Tommy nodded, but he was not too thrilled about it. What would Sharon say about him bringing home a bag full of dodgy money?

Ronnie reached into his dressing gown pocket and produced a roll of notes and peeled off a wad of crisp fifties.

"There is a grand here, Tommy my son. There will be another waiting for you Wednesday when you deliver. Okay?'

The sight of the money alleviated some of Tommy's fears as he took it and put it in his jacket pocket.

"Right then. Any questions?" asked Ronnie as he drained his coffee cup.

Tommy saw this as a cue to get moving.

"No, Ronnie. I will text you when I have the key."

Ronnie led Tommy to the door once more with his arm draped around his shoulder. It felt heavy.

"Good man. You'll be fine. Off you go and keep me updated. My phone will always be on. Oh, and if for some reason anything goes pear shaped or not to plan, I want to know right away. Get it?"

Tommy felt a surge of adrenaline in his belly.

"Yes, I understand."

Once outside, Tommy looked back at the house, but the door was already shut.

He got into his car.

He was apprehensive about the job and the degree of responsibility it brought to bear on his shoulders. The amount of money in the bag frightened the crap out of him. But the wages he was being paid were good and Sharon would be well happy.

He wanted her to be proud of him. He had let her down so many times before.

Tommy started up the engine and put the radio on.

The 90's song *Things Can Only Get Better* by D:Ream was playing.

It brought a smile to his face, and he immediately felt better.

He would do this job. No problem.

If he kept his nerve and followed it to the letter, it would be fine.

What could possibly go wrong?

Chapter 3

Tommy Scott parked his car in a side road a little distance from the hotel and decided to walk the rest of the way on foot. He didn't want his car on CCTV in the car park of the Marriott.

He had spoken on the phone a little while ago to this Joseph Caine and they had agreed to meet in the hotel bar at twelve noon sharp.

It had begun to rain again so Tommy put on his overcoat.

The coat was a bit of a moth-eaten thing and he had meant to buy a new one this winter, but money had been tight.

Also, he still liked it.

Sharon had bought it for him as a Christmas present some years ago now not long after they were married. It had snowed on Boxing Day and he could remember wearing it as they walked in the local park and admired the wintery scenery.

Happy days.

Days Tommy really wanted back.

The coat may be tatty, but it was still functional.

At least it would keep his suit dry until he got inside the hotel.

* * *

Ten minutes later, he stood in the foyer of the hotel and took off his coat. He quickly found the bathroom and combed his hair and dried his face with a paper towel.

Tommy regarded himself in the mirror above the sink. He looked passable.

He was still a good-looking man, but the ravishes of drugs and drink had aged him.

Maybe after this job, things would become more stable for him and he could look after himself better.

He owed that to Sharon.

This money could go towards a nice holiday. It had been an age since they had gone abroad. In fact, it had been ages since they had a proper holiday of any sort. They had both fancied the Greek Islands, but had never been. Maybe now was the time?

Satisfied with one last look at his appearance, he headed for the bar and took no time in spotting Joseph Caine sat on a bar stool sipping on what looked like a scotch.

Tommy hadn't been into a bar for a while now. The brightly coloured optics and beer pumps seemed to call out to him, trying to seduce him. Maybe meeting here wasn't such a smart move.

He licked his lips, but told himself to focus on what he was here to do.

Joseph Caine saw him approaching and recognised him also from a photo image. He swivelled on his stool to face Tommy.

Both men appraised each other before Caine offered his hand.

"I'm Joseph. You must be Tommy?"

Tommy shook the offered hand.

"Nice to meet you, Joseph."

"Would you like a drink?" Caine offered.

Every fibre of Tommy's being screamed *yes, I fucking would love a drink*, but he somehow resisted.

"No thanks."

Caine nodded.

"Okay, let's get down to business."

He produced from his pocket a receipt and a silver key with a red fob on it. The words *Luggage Safe* were printed on it in small lettering and the number 79.

"Here's the key and receipt. The bag is in *Luggage Safe* at the back of *News Plus* just outside the railway station. Name is Walter White if they ask, but they probably won't as long as you have the key and receipt. That's it."

Tommy never reacted to the name. He picked up the items and regarded Caine.

"It is all there, is it? The money, I mean."

Joseph Caine smiled and swallowed his drink in one gulp. He then got off of the bar stool. He was a good six inches taller than Tommy.

"Don't fucking insult me, Tommy. I am a pro. The bag was deposited untouched, as requested. My boss, Mr Doyle, has the upmost respect for your Mr Moon. They have done business many times. They go a long way back. Even if I wanted to, I would be a fool to tamper with the money. I would be a dead man. So would you."

Caine's eyes bored into Tommy's, suddenly making him feel uncomfortable.

"Sorry, Joseph. It was a stupid thing to say. This is the first time I've done this sort of thing. I'm a little twitchy."

Caine's face suddenly split into a smile.

"Okay, Tommy. Apology accepted."

He sat back down on the stool and beckoned the bartender over.

"You sure I can't tempt you, Tommy? Settle those nerves?"

Tommy watched Caine's glass be refilled with the single malt.

"Go on then. I'll have a quick one."

Tommy sat onto the stool next to Caine and ordered a double.

* * *

Tommy walked out of the hotel thirty minutes later. He had only had two drinks and he was mighty proud of that fact. It had tasted like nectar, and it went down as smooth as honey.

He checked in the pocket of his overcoat and felt the key and receipt safely there.

The rain had now gone off and a watery sun was poking its head through the clouds.

He decided to walk to the station. It wasn't far. Parking there would be a right pain in the ass. Plus, once more, it would keep his car out of the public eye and CCTV.

Tommy would come back for it later. It was only a short walk, and his car was safe where it was.

* * *

Walking past a bar-come-café named *Patti's*, he heard his name being called.

Tommy looked to the collection of outside tables and chairs and spotted who it was that was trying to get his attention.

It was an old school chum and friend, Finlay Bryant.

It had been a few years since he had last seen him.

They had been tight just like brothers, but when both got married, things started to drift.

Finlay had gone back to Dublin, his place of birth, to live for a while with his new Bride, Angela, but things hadn't worked out and he had returned to Bristol.

Tommy had rekindled his relationship with him, but Sharon wasn't keen because Finlay was a pothead and a piss artist to boot. He was a bad influence on Tommy.

When the Covid pandemic came along, it once more disrupted their friendship and it had been around two years since they had last met. Sharon had been glad that they had been split up again.

Tommy knew he was a liability, but he had missed his old friend.

"Tomo, you old scrot. How are you, my man?" shouted Finlay.

He had already sunk a few by the look of him and the empty bottles on the table he occupied.

Tommy made his way to the table and embraced his friend.

"Shit, Fin! It's been ages! You been keeping alright?"

"Yes, man. Sound. What are you doing around here, dressed as if you have just come out of court?"

Tommy was cagey with his reply.

"Just doing a few chores in town. That's all."

He quickly changed the subject before his friend could probe more.

"Are you still living in Stokes Croft?"

"Yeah. I'm still renting that dive in Herald Way, but it's dirt cheap and there's a pub on the corner. Heaven. You still with Sharon?"

"Yes, we are sweet."

Finlay got to his feet.

"Fuck, it's so good to see you. I have loads to tell you. Have you got time for a drink?"

Tommy hesitated. He needed to pick up the bag.

"Come on, Tom. For fuck's sake, one won't kill you. It's been an age,' said Fin.

He was right. It had been an age since he had seen Fin and decided one wouldn't hurt.

The taste of the whiskey was still tantalizing his tongue from earlier. One more would be okay.

* * *

Five hours later found the two men wolfing down Big Mac meals.

They were sat on a bench overlooking the dockside. Both propped each other up as they were well and truly wrecked.

Tommy's suit was in a dishevelled state and his tie and shirt front bore the stains of ketchup and mayonnaise.

Tommy had fallen off the wagon spectacularly.

After the first drink that Fin had bought, a switch seemed to flick inside Tommy and there was no turning back. He had pressed the self-destruct button.

An afternoon of drinking export-strength lager, whiskey chasers and smoking some good quality puff later had triggered their hunger, so here they were now.

As they finished off their food, Finlay stood up and brazenly urinated in the nearby bushes.

Zipping himself back up, he said, "Tom. We'll make our way to the *Green Man*. Remember Skipper and Bushy? They drink in there regularly. They would love to see you. They will be in tonight for sure."

Tommy nodded drunkenly.

Barry Skipton and Craig Bush had always hung out with them back in the day and had shared their passion for music. They went to many a gig together over the years.

Tommy got up off the bench on the third attempt.

Suddenly, through his alcohol and drug-fuddled haze, he remembered the key and he frantically felt for it in his pocket. It was thankfully still there.

He pulled out his mobile and looked at the time. 6:00pm.

Luggage Safe closed for the day an hour ago. Shit.

He then saw three miscalls from Ronnie and then a couple of voicemails.

Tommy played them.

Tommy, this is Ronnie. Did the meet go ok? Have you got the bag? Get back to me asap.

The second one was an hour later.

Tommy, you fucking muppet. Do I need to be worrying? Answer your phone and let me know all is alright.

Tommy felt his stomach churn.

He had done what he hoped he wouldn't do. He had fucked up royally.

Once he got on the bevvy, all thoughts of why he was in Bristol city centre and the job at hand went right out of his head.

He was a complete twat.

He was weak.

The lure of the booze had enveloped him again.

But he could salvage this.

Finlay staggered over to him.

"Are we going or what?"

"Yeah. In a minute."

Tommy managed to text Ronnie.

All good. Phone died on me and I had to buy a new charger. Job done and I have the bag. It will be with you tomorrow. Sorry for delay.

His hands shook as he looked at the screen and checked the spelling.

Satisfied, he hit the send button.

It would be okay. He had the receipt and key. He would go there first thing in the morning and retrieve the bag and be back at Ronnie's by lunch time. No sweat. In fact, it was better that he was not carrying the bag around with him.

Not in this state.

Shame washed over him again as he thought what Sharon would think of him after her going out on a limb to get him this job.

His phone buzzed.

It was Ronnie.

Thank fuck for that. You had me going for a moment. See you tomorrow and keep that bag safe. It is of prime importance to me.

Tommy breathed a sigh of relief.

"Are you coming or not?" asked Fin.

The alcohol had now given Tommy bravado and a touch of Dutch courage.

Fuck Ronnie and this money.

He would have a fucking good night and get the bag to Ronnie tomorrow and he would be none the wiser.

"Right, let's go meet the boys and get some serious drinking in."

As he walked after Finlay, he managed a text to Sharon, telling her the job was running late and he wouldn't be back to the small hours and not to wait up.

Chapter 4

Tommy tried to open his eyes, but they felt as if they had been superglued shut. As he slowly awoke, his head pounded like crazy and his mouth felt like the inside of an old sock.

Shit, what a night.

He remembered finally stumbling out of the pub and into a taxi back to his house about two o'clock in the morning.

His car had been forgotten about during the course of the evening, not that he had any chance of driving it.

Ravenously hungry, he had made his way into the kitchen and decided he fancied some toast. He managed to put two slices of bread in the toaster and turned it up to full heat as he didn't want to wait too long.

He had sat down at the kitchen table while they cooked and had fallen asleep. Tommy had then abruptly woken due to the smoke alarm going off and the smell of burnt toast.

Next, he was confronted by a fuming Sharon who called him all the irresponsible, useless bastards under the sun.

He had sat there like a dummy and just taken the abuse. He deserved it. He had been a complete ass and had blown all the trust Sharon had built up in him over the last few months and had knocked a big hole in the grand that Ronnie had given him that previous day.

He hung his head in shame as Sharon told him he would be sleeping on the sofa and stormed back to bed.

Tommy had finally stood up and staggered into the hall and attempted to hang his overcoat up on a peg, but after half a dozen attempts, it just ended up on the floor. He couldn't be bothered to pick it back up.

The last thing he could recall was collapsing face down on the sofa fully clothed and crashed out into oblivion.

Tommy now sat up. Suddenly, he was hit by a wave of nausea. He sat still until it passed.

Eventually peeling his eyes open, he squinted at the mantlepiece clock: 11.00am.

Christ, Ronnie would be going ape shit expecting his money.

He pulled out his phone from his trouser pocket. The battery was dead.

Tommy got up unsteadily onto his feet and wandered over to the sideboard. He pulled open the top drawer and rummaged in it until he found a phone charger. He plugged it in and then headed into the kitchen to make a cup of coffee.

The charred remains of his toast were still in the toaster. A sad reminder of last night and the whole shameful debacle.

As he waited for the kettle to boil, he slowly made his way upstairs to the bedroom.

The door was wide open and the bed was made. There was no sign of Sharon. No doubt she had gone to work.

It was going to be a long way back for him and their relationship.

What a prat.

Back downstairs, he made a strong black coffee and went back into the living room. He checked his phone, which now had a small bit of charge on it, and saw to his horror four miscalls from Ronnie. *Shit.*

He would drink this coffee and hit the shower and then drive back to fetch the money and head up to Ronnie's.

No, that wasn't going to work.

His car was still parked in the side street by the hotel from yesterday.

Fuck.

Everything seemed simple last night. Now in the reality of the next morning, he was panicking.

Fucking Finlay Bryant.

He knew he shouldn't have stopped for that drink with him.

Ronnie was not going to be happy. He would have to concoct some tale to get himself out of this. Maybe if he was clever enough, he might get away with it. If so, the rest of his payment might go some way to pacify Sharon. Maybe.

Tommy now thought of the key and went into the hallway. He looked at the pegs on the wall. There were four of them. Three were empty and the fourth one had a purple woollen scarf of Sharon's hung on it.

He then remembered trying to hang up the coat with no success and it ending up on the floor. He stared at the carpet, but there was nothing there.

Maybe I got it wrong?

Confused, he went back into the living room and scouted around, but with no success.

No, wait a minute. He had definitely put it in the hall. He was sure of this.

Back out in the hall, he stood staring at the threadbare carpet, hoping somehow the coat would reappear as if by magic.

Maybe Sharon had picked it up and put it in the wardrobe.

With a knot of anxiousness gradually growing in his stomach, he went upstairs to their bedroom and searched the wardrobe without any luck.

Tommy now searched the house high and low, but there was no sign of it.

The anxiousness he was feeling now turned to dread.

Where the fuck was the coat?

He felt himself break out in a cold sweat and nausea washed over him again.

Come on. Think, Tommy. Think.

Sharon. He would call Sharon. She wouldn't like him calling her at work and he hoped to God she would answer.

He checked her work rota stuck to the fridge door and saw she was on shift at 12.30pm.

Looking at his watch, he saw the time was 12.10pm.

He grabbed his phone, which was now fifty percent charged, and rang her number.

She answered after half a dozen rings.

"Go away, Tommy. I don't want to talk to you. I'm about to start work so get lost."

Tommy panicked.

"Wait. Don't put the phone down. I need to ask you something."

"If it's for forgiveness you can forget it, Tommy Scott. You have abused my trust yet again and…"

Tommy cut her off in mid-sentence.

"Shut the fuck up, Shar. I know what I am and what I've done, but right now, answer me this. Have you seen my overcoat?"

Sharon was momentarily taken aback.

"Overcoat? What overcoat?"

"My old one that usually hangs in the hall. I wore it yesterday and took it off last night when I came home. I think it dropped on the floor."

There was a moment's silence as Sharon thought.

"Oh, that old thing. I saw it this morning on top of those bin liners full of stuff for the charity shop. I thought that scruffy, old coat was to go as well."

Tommy felt his blood freeze in his veins. He clutched the door frame to steady himself. When he spoke, his voice was a croak.

"Are you saying you took the coat to a charity shop? My coat?"

Sharon answered with irritation back in her voice.

"Yes. What does it matter? It's motheaten. Get yourself a new one."

"You took the coat without asking me?"

"Yes. I took it. You weren't in any fit state to ask this morning. What's the big deal, anyway?"

Tommy thought he was going to pass out.

"You stupid fucking bitch. Do you know what you've done?"

Sharon was taken aback by Tommy's aggressiveness.

"Now you just hang fire, Tommy. You don't speak to me like that."

Tommy cut her down again.

"Which charity shop? Where?"

"What?" exclaimed Sharon.

"You heard. Which charity shop?"

"It was on the high street. The *Blue Cross,* I think?"

Tommy felt his world shrinking.

"What do you mean 'you think'? Was it the *Blue Cross* or not?"

The venom in his voice now frightened Sharon.

"Yes. Yes, it was. The one next door to the *Tesco Metro.* What's wrong, Tommy?"

"What time did you bring the bags into the shop?"

"Ah, 11.30am. What the hell is going on?"

She was answered by silence as Tommy hung up the call and headed for the front door.

Chapter 5

Adam Lucas sat on the pavement outside *McDonald's*. He was wrapped up in a swarth of dirty blankets.

He wore a beanie hat pulled tightly down on his head and a pair of tatty fingerless gloves, but this didn't stop the bitterly cold November wind cutting through him like a knife.

Rubbing his hand over a week's growth of beard, he knew it was time to get up and move to another spot.

The manager of the betting shop next door would be here soon to open, and he hated Adam with a passion and would be phoning the law as soon as he spotted him.

Adam had done alright so far today. Passers-by had dropped enough money in his empty paper cup for him to buy a bacon and egg McMuffin meal and a coffee.

For now, his belly was full. It was the cold that was bothering him.

If he was to stay outside all day, he was going to have to find some more layers to wear or risk hypothermia.

Adam saw the black BMW pull up next door and he quickly got to his feet.

With his blankets wrapped around him and cup in hand, he headed off down the road before the manager of the betting shop got out of his vehicle.

He cursed as he felt the first drops of rain.

It had been miserable weather all month, especially for those out on the streets. November so far had been grey, cold and wet.

Adam walked along thinking about where to head next. Maybe he would go to *Sainsbury's Local* further on into the town centre and sit by the ATM machines outside the store. There was always some likely soul or sucker, depending on how you looked at it, that would give him a few quid.

As the rain got heavier, Adam shivered miserably. His jacket just wasn't keeping out the cold.

He was passing the *Blue Cross* charity shop when he decided to go inside. In his paper cup, he had £5.50. Surely, he could get something to keep him warm for that.

Dropping his blankets outside on the pavement, he went in. Immediately, he was hit by the warmth of the heaters in the shop. It was the sort of heat that, after coming in from the cold, would made your cheeks glow red and burn. One such heater was directly overhead as you entered, and Adam could have happily stayed in that spot all day.

He made his way towards the men's clothing, which he mused was always the smallest section in a charity shop and nine times out of ten tucked away at the rear.

Usually, you would find an assortment of clothes that had been worn either by a deceased eighty-year-old or some tasteless colourblind forty something, size XXL. Then there was always an endless rack of garish ties and a variety of worn belts. No chance of finding any items from *Burton*, *Fat Face* or *Next*.

The lady serving at the counter furtively watched him. Her name badge attached to her pink cardigan covering her ample breasts read *Pat Manager*. Adam smiled to himself. Was that her name or an invitation?

As he walked past the counter, she wrinkled her nose in distaste. He couldn't blame her. He was dishevelled and smelly, not the sort of customer she desired in her shop.

For her, charity began at home and obviously not in here.

Adam ignored her and went to the gent's clothing and started looking at the jumpers, hoping to find a decent hoodie or sweatshirt.

Just then from the back room came another member of staff. This lady had a kindly face and reminded him of his grandmother.

"Morning, love," she said to him as she hung an overcoat onto the rail.

She looked at her watch and corrected herself.

"Oh, or should I say good afternoon. My, it's gone twelve already."

Adam smiled at her.

She now looked more closely at him.

"You look perished, my dear. This coat that I just hung up here would do you a treat."

Adam looked at it. Although it was well worn, it would still be warm.

"How much is it?" he asked.

The woman regarded him and then the paper cup in his hand.

"What have you got in that cup?"

"£5.50."

The woman smiled.

"Well, what do you know? That's the price exactly."

Adam smiled. He knew deep down the coat would be priced more, but he would accept this generous gesture from this lovely lady who was not judgemental in any way towards him.

Adam tipped the money out of the cup into her hand, apologising and brushing away a dead bug that came with the coins.

The lady gave him the coat and he immediately put it on. It fitted well. Perfect.

"Would you like a receipt?" asked the other lady at the till.

Adam smiled.

"No, thanks. I'll write this off as tax deductible with my accountant."

As he left the shop, he noticed the rain had got even harder.

This wasn't the day he had planned.

Adam picked up his blankets. He then pulled up the collar on his new coat and headed off down the high street.

Eventually, he came to a small inner city link train station. He walked into the car park and looked around. It was quiet. Adam glanced back to see if anybody had seen him enter the car park. Everything seemed okay.

Reaching into his jeans pocket, he produced a set of car keys.

Walking towards a silver Datsun, he pushed the key fob and the car doors opened.

Adam bundled the blankets into the boot and then jumped into the driver's seat. Hopefully, the weather tomorrow would be better and he would give it another go.

Time to head home to warm up and have a nice cup of tea.

***

Adam pulled the car up on the driveway outside a terraced house in an area of Bristol called Fishponds, which was about three miles from where he had parked at the station.

He got out and walked up to the front door. The blue paint was peeling off of it. The whole house needed painting, but that cost money. Money, he didn't have.

Entering the house, he heard the sounds of the television and he walked into the living room to find his wife Jackie, who was six months pregnant, sat on the floor on a yoga mat stretching while watching *Escape to the Country*. They both hoped one day they would be in a position to do this.

"Hello, love," called Adam.

Jackie turned around and smiled.

"You're back early," she said.

"Rain stopped play, I'm afraid. Plus, it's bloody freezing out there."

Jackie laughed and pushed her blonde hair away from her attractive face.

"Hence the trendy new overcoat, I take it."

Adam looked down at the coat.

"Yes indeed. A bargain for £5.50."

He moved to his wife and made to kiss her.

She flinched away.

"No chance, Mr. Go have a shower and put those clothes in the garage."

Adam feigned total shock.

"Also, when is that horrible beard going?"

It was Adam's turn to laugh.

"Not yet, my sweet. I have another few days yet. We creative types must suffer for our art. Look at Byron, Van Gogh and Oscar Wilde."

"I am not interested in them, just my husband. Now get in the shower. You stink."

Adam threw up a mock salute.

"Yes, Mam."

As he headed out the room, he turned back.

"How is junior today?"

Jackie put her hands on her tummy.

"Kicking like bloody Ronaldo."

"Well, if he comes out half the footballer Ronaldo is, we'll be set for life."

"I hope so," replied Jackie, "The electric bill is on the kitchen table and it doesn't make great reading."

Adam grimaced and headed for the stairs.

Sodding bills.

In the shower, Adam let the hot spray work all over him, the cold in his bones eventually residing. He shampooed his hair and then soaped himself clean with shower gel. Drying himself with a warm towel, he thanked God that he wasn't really homeless.

He was working on a book. A fictional tale that evolved around a person living rough on the streets. Adam wanted to experience what it was like to be on the streets so that he could write the story more authentically. This book was important for him. No, more than important. Fucking crucial.

He was a burgeoning writer who had experienced moderate success writing articles for a free local newspaper and then he had done a few commissions for a couple of mainstream magazines, but ultimately, he wanted to be an author.

Up to now, he had little success, so this book was make or break for him and for his wife Jackie and their first unborn child.

Jackie had a decent job as a paramedic, but when the baby was born, she wanted to be a stay-at-home full-time mum. She loved kids and wanted more sooner rather than later as she was 27 years of age and her biological clock was ticking.

This put pressure on Adam to start earning an income from his writing or he was going to have to go out into the real world, according to his dad, and get a proper job.

Adam had previously worked in IT, but it had bored the crap out of him.

From a young age, he had been an avid reader and then he had turned his hand to writing stories. He envied the writers of today, James Patterson, Stephen King, J.K. Rowling and their like, making a lucrative living from their passion.

Adam was determined not to go backwards to a dead-end job. But the bills and the debts were piling up.

A couple of publishers expressed interest in his proposed story, but needed a synopsis and a few sample chapters before committing. So, armed with what he thought was a great plot for a novel, he had taken to the streets over the last few weeks at various times of night and day to live the character he had created.

It had been an eyeopener, to say the least, and he had ultimate respect for the people living outside 24/7, especially in the winter months.

So far, he had survived the conditions by staying outside for a certain amount of time and then he would secretively head home.

He had stayed out at night a few times, but it had become decidedly dodgy. The night people were a different breed and you didn't want to piss them off or tread on their patch.

He had experienced a few scrapes, but managed to talk his way out of them unscathed.

Any money he made usually went back to a local charity. He didn't keep it.

A few more days, or maybe a week more, would give him enough material and then he needed to sit down in front of his laptop and get writing.

Money was already tight.

Doing out the spare room as a nursery and buying all the bits and pieces you need for a newborn had stretched them to their limits. Keeping the car on the road and putting petrol in it was now becoming a battle, especially at present with the situation between Ukraine and Russia and rising oil prices. Never mind the price of electric and gas.

They used to own two cars, but now they were down to just the Datsun.

Their last holiday had been three years ago.

Their parents helped out when they could, but there was only so many times you could ask to lend money before your pride kicked in or just plain embarrassment.

The book had to work. Their livelihood depended on it.

As Adam pulled on a t-shirt and tracksuit bottoms, Jackie's voice sounded from the bottom of the stairs.

"Adam, I'm going around Mum's for a while. Have you got the car keys?"

Adam cringed, remembering the fuel gauge was almost on red when he pulled up. Hopefully, there would be enough petrol for Jackie to get there and back.

"I'll get them. I think they're in the pocket of that magnificent overcoat I bought."

Going into the bedroom, Adam headed to the pile of disregarded clothes. Jackie was right. They stunk. He would have to put them out in the garage.

Picking up the overcoat, he rummaged in the pockets until he found the keys. As he did this, he felt something else, but it had gone into the lining. He felt it again it.

Was it another key?

Jackie appeared at the bedroom door.

"Have you found them?"

"Here you go, love."

Adam handed them over.

"Drive safely and give my love to Lynda."

Jackie took the keys.

"Will do. What are your plans for the rest of the afternoon?"

"Not sure," replied Adam.

"Well, the kitchen sink seems like it's blocked as the water is running away slowly. Maybe take a look at it."

Adam grinned at his wife.

"Terrific."

Once Jackie had gone, Adam went back to the coat and felt the lining until he found what he thought was a key once more. He discovered a small hole in the pocket's lining and worked it bigger with his fingers until he could grab the object.

It was a key.

Adam held it up and examined it.

The key looked like it came from a locker.

It had a bright red fob on it and the number 79.

He had seen a key like this before, but where?

Adam studied it some more and then searched the pockets of the coat again and found a piece of paper. On reading it, he found it was a receipt.

Luggage Safe. Temple Way. Bristol.

Of course. That's how he recognised the key. His good mate, Leon Biggs, worked there as the manager.

When things went stale with his writing, Adam would often pop down there on Leon's lunchbreak for a coffee and a chat.

They had met at college back in the day and had hit it off immediately as they both had a passion for Marvel Comics and the whole superhero thing. When the big film franchise came to the cinema with the likes of the Hulk, Iron Man and the Avengers, all their dreams had come true at once to see their comic book heroes up on the silver screen. Both still had a large collection of comics and never tired of getting together and chatting about them.

Earlier this year, Leon had been promoted to manager, so he was in a position to let Adam come around to the back of the shop to see how the operation worked. That's how Adam had seen loads of these keys before. Now he was curious why one was left in this coat, but the writer in him was even more curious to find out what was in locker 79.

It was like a film plot. What mystery was in locker 79?

He checked the coat thoroughly, but found nothing else in the pockets or lining and no name in the collar.

Adam reasoned if the coat ended up in the charity shop, either the owner wasn't aware the key had been in it or they had made an error and the coat went into the shop by mistake. They would probably come looking for it at the *Blue Cross* shop, but there was no trace of him buying it.

The right thing to do was to return the coat and the key to the shop and explain what had happened and hope the rightful owner would retrieve it, but he was curious to see what was in that locker.

It wouldn't hurt.

Just a bit of fun and intrigue.

Like the Famous Five or Hardy Boys story plots he used to read as a youngster.

It could be nothing. No more than somebody's dirty laundry or a briefcase full of tax returns.

It was worth a look and if it wasn't the crown jewels, he would return the coat with the key intact back to the *Blue Cross*. No harm done.

If Leon was working today, he would open it for him. He was sure of that.

Leon had been known to pull a few strokes in his time and wasn't exactly squeaky clean. As a kid, he had stolen a car or two on more than one occasion and done a bit of shop lifting.

Would Adam have time to do this before Jackie came back?

He would have to get a bus to town.

Also, what about the kitchen sink?

Jackie would be pissed off if he hadn't sorted it out by the time she came back.

Still, the intrigue was too much.

Pocketing the key and receipt safely, Adam headed out.

As he walked to the bus stop, he texted Leon asking if he was at work. A couple of minutes later, a return text came through.

"Yes, I am here until 5.00pm. What's up?"

Chapter 6

Tommy pulled the E-scooter into the kerb. He had picked one up on the corner of his street. It had been the last one and he thanked God it had been working.

It had made short work of his arrival on Gloucester Road, his local high street, and he soon found the *Blue Cross* shop.

Gloucester Road is located in North Bristol and runs through the areas of St Andrews, Bishopton and Horfield. It has a large number of independent traders, as well as household named shops. There are also a great choice of cafés, bars and restaurants for when a rest is needed. It is a real quirky and Bohemian addition to Bristol's shopping areas and is very popular amongst a cross section of ages.

Even though the November afternoon was bitterly cold, Tommy was sweating as he headed to the shop. His head still felt like he had a marching band playing in there, but he tried to ignore it.

He checked his phone. Two miscalls from Sharon and three from Ronnie.

Tommy hoped and prayed that the coat would still be here. He didn't want to contemplate the thought that it wouldn't be.

Once inside the charity shop, he soon found the men's section. It was relatively quiet in there. He rummaged through a rack with a small selection of coats on it, but his wasn't there.

Tommy now headed for the counter where a rather snooty-looking woman stood filing her nails.

She saw him coming.

"Yes, may I be of help?"

Her voice didn't really echo her request.

"Yes. Earlier, my wife brought a few bags of items in here and, by mistake, she put my overcoat in it. I wonder if you may still have it."

"Overcoat, you say. I don't recall. Ah, wait a moment."

She called across to an elderly lady who was putting books on a shelf.

"Jean, didn't you sell an overcoat this morning?"

Jean stopped what she was doing and looked to the ceiling as if the answer might be written there.

"Why yes, I did. I sold it to the homeless guy. You know, the young fellow that we have seen up and down the street the last month or so. The poor dear was freezing. He was happy as Larry when he left wearing it. He..."

The other woman cut her short.

"Right. Thanks, Jean. That was very helpful."

Jean huffed due to the fact of being shut up and returned to stacking the shelf.

Pat Hargreaves, the manageress, was a right stroppy mare. Paraded around here like she was the Queen.

She now looked at the man.

"I'm sorry, sir, but it has been bought."

She saw the look of despair on his face.

"It was ours to sell, you know. We had no idea that it was brought in by mistake."

Tommy took a deep breath to control his rising anger. He felt like his head was about to explode.

"Do you keep a record of who buys things in here?"

'Well, if they are a taxpayer and wish to donate to Gift Aid, then we would have their name; otherwise, no."

"I don't suppose the person who bought the coat..."

Pat intervened.

"Certainly not. He was a homeless person. Hardly a tax payer."

Tommy felt his heart sink. He was a dead man.

Panic rose inside him.

"This person who bought it, you mentioned he frequents this street daily?"

Pat looked towards Jean again.

"Jean, do you know this chap who bought the coat?"

Jean begrudgingly put down the book she had in her hand.

She noticed ironically that it was a dog-eared copy of Jackie Collins' *The Bitch*.

Jean walked over to the man.

"I don't know him personally, but when I have been out shopping, I have seen him. Usually, he's outside *McDonald's* or *Costa*."

"What does he look like?" asked Tommy.

Jean looked to the ceiling again.

"Well, he must be in his early to mid-thirties. He has long brown hair tied in a ponytail and a full beard. Today when he bought your coat, he was wearing a black beanie hat. I believe there was an image of one of those superhero fellows that my Grandson absolutely loves on the front of it. Oh, what's he called? Ah, Batman. No, that's wrong. Spiderman. Yes, that's it. Spiderman."

Tommy digested the information. He asked for a pen and paper and wrote down his name and mobile number.

"If by any chance this guy comes back in with the coat or anything he may have found in it, please immediately ring me. It is really important. Also, if you see him in the street, tell him you have a customer that will pay £20 to him for his coat back."

Tommy headed to the door and his first port of call: *McDonald's*.

As he was leaving, the woman behind the counter called out.

"What is he likely to find in the coat, may I ask?"

Tommy ignored her and walked out.

His trip to *McDonald's* turned up nothing, nor did his visit to *Costa*. He walked up and down the road with no success until he spotted somebody sat outside the *Halifax* bank.

Tommy sprinted up to them. They were wrapped in blankets sleeping, so he couldn't see them properly.

Tommy was in no mood to mess about. He grabbed the person and shook them awake. He immediately recoiled as he saw it was a woman in her late fifties or early sixties. He couldn't tell from her weather-beaten features.

Tommy mumbled an apology as he saw the look of fear in her eyes. He dropped her a fiver and headed back to the scooter.

Fuck it, he would go to *Luggage Safe* and explain the situation. He somehow remembered Joseph Caine had said he booked the bag in under the name of Walter White.

He hadn't said anything at the time, but he knew that was the name of that geezer in the television series *Breaking Bad*. Plus, he knew the key was number 79.

He couldn't afford to waste any more time hanging around here all day waiting to see if this dude would turn up.

Starting up the scooter, he headed down the road towards the city centre. The traffic would be bad at this time of day, but he had no other choice. He had to get the bag. He dare not risk going home until he did.

He also hoped this man who had got his coat hadn't found the key or figured out what it was he had. He didn't even want to contemplate that.

Also, if he didn't answer Ronnie's call soon, he knew his brother-in-law would be on his way down to Bristol for a visit. That thought sent a chill down his spine.

Nobody sane wanted a house call from Ronnie 'Barking at the' Moon.

Chapter 7

"Do you still have sugar in your coffee?"

"Yeah. One, please."

Leon Biggs spooned sugar into a mug bearing the logo of the Avengers and handed it to Adam.

They were both in Leon's office at the rear of *Luggage Safe*.

Adam was sat on a small sofa.

Leon grabbed his own mug and sat behind his small, untidy desk.

The desk reflected its owner, a person not particularly organised or disciplined in life.

"So, how are things? It's been a while. Written that bestseller yet?"

Adam laughed.

"Not yet, but I have an idea for one and a publisher interested."

Leon's eyes widened.

"Oh yeah. Can you reveal the plot?"

Adam took a sip of coffee.

"Nope. But I have been out the past month regularly living on the streets to get a taste of what I want to write about."

Leon nodded.

"That explains why you look like a missing member of the Blue Oyster Cult."

Adam stroked his beard.

"Got to look the part. Another week or so and it will be gone, and the hair will also be cut."

"How's the delectable Jackie, may I ask?"

"Beautiful, but looking more like a beach ball every day."

Leon dunked a chocolate hobnob into his coffee.

"How long is it now?"

Adam watched as his friend put the whole soggy biscuit in his mouth in one bite.

"She is six months yesterday."

"Wow! Soon, you'll be a daddy. Good for you."

Leon reached for another biscuit.

"So, Leon how is Maureen?"

Maureen had been Leon's on/off girlfriend for the past three years.

"Oh, she's looking like a beach ball more and more each day as well."

Adam raised his eyebrows.

Leon smiled.

"No, she isn't pregnant; it's just all the chocolate bars, cakes, crisps and pizzas she demolishes on a daily basis. She eats enough food to keep a third-world country supplied for a year. Exercise to Mo is getting off the sofa and making it to the fridge."

Adam laughed.

He knew Maureen was a big girl, but then again, Leon was not exactly skinny himself. They both shared a love of food and films. They were a perfect match made in heaven. They just didn't realise it. Both just too selfish sometimes to invest in their relationship.

Leon reached for another biscuit.

"Anyway, this isn't just a social visit. You mentioned a key over the phone?"

Adam had thought how he was going to play this on the journey over. He didn't want to involve his friend in anything illegal. So, he decided to keep the truth about the key to himself.

"I've come to collect from one of your lockers," said Adam.

Leon went for the fourth biscuit.

"You should have mentioned to me you were going to store something here. I would have given you a good discount."

"Well, it was all a bit last minute, to be honest. I've bought some special bits and pieces for the baby and Jackie. The trouble is there is nowhere in our house to hide stuff and Jackie at present is obsessed with cleaning and tiding up and I was paranoid she would find them, so I decided to store them safely until I was ready to give them to her. I didn't have a clue where to put them, then I thought of here. It's ideal."

"Right," nodded Leon.

Adam continued, hoping he sounded convincing.

"When I came down to store the items, you weren't around, so I thought when I picked them up again, I would see if you were available for a cuppa and a catch-up. You know, we should all go out for dinner soon. I heard the *Golden Sun* does cracking Chinese food."

The talk of food seemed to distract Leon.

"Yes. Definitely, mate. Maureen would love that."

"Okay. That's a date. I'll run it by Jackie tonight. Anyway, sorry it's a flying visit, but I have one hundred and one things to do."

Leon got up from his desk looking longingly at the half-eaten packet of hobnobs.

"Right, let's get your things. Got your key and receipt handy?"

* * *

Five minutes later, Adam waited nervously at the counter, not sure what to expect. He glanced furtively around, imagining at any moment that he would feel a hand on his shoulder and it would be the rightful owner of key 79.

Leon then appeared carrying a black holdall.

"There we go. All safe, sound and intact."

He placed the bag on the counter.

The bag had a security tag through the zipper with a name on it.

Leon read it.

"Walter White?" he looked puzzled.

Adam laughed.

"I know it sounds stupid, but all the cloak and dagger stuff got me excited and I thought I would use a fake name for a bit of fun."

Leon laughed.

"Fucking hell. Why old Walt White? I thought it would be Peter Parker or Bruce Banner, maybe even Tony Stark. Paying homage to our Marvel heroes."

Luckily, Adam had been a big fan of the *Breaking Bad* show.

"The name just isn't obvious unless you really know the show. I thought it was a bit more subtle."

Leon seemed suitably satisfied with the explanation.

"You'll be telling me next the bag is full of crystal meth rocks."

Both men laughed.

"There's a private room around the back if you want to check out your contents before leaving. Once you take it away, we claim no responsibility for the bag or what's in it. It hasn't been molested in anyway, but I always advise customers to check before going. Then there are no comebacks."

Adam suddenly felt a pang of guilt.

What if the contents of the bag was somebody's holiday clothes or a birthday present? He couldn't just take that away. It wouldn't be right. Plus, he would have no use for it.

So, although he wanted to get away as quickly as possible, he opted for the secure room to see what was exactly in the bag.

What did he expect to find anyway?

Well, if it was somebody's personal items, he could just check the bag back in and walk away from it. No harm done. Just make an excuse to Leon.

Leon showed him to the room.

"It locks from the inside. Take your time. We give customers fifteen minutes before we come back and knock the door. The room is totally private, no cameras present."

Once Leon had left, Adam locked the door with shaking hands. His adrenaline was bubbling, and his curiosity spiked.

Why hadn't he just handed the key in to Leon and told him the truth? Or better still, returned the coat and its contents to the *Blue Cross* shop where he purchased it.

It was the curiosity that had hooked him.

Anyway, he could still return the bag and key and walk away, no harm done.

Adam moved to the bag.

He had trouble undoing the tag on the zipper, but eventually managed.

As he eased back the zipper, his phone rang. He pulled it out and looked at the screen. It was Jackie. He thought about not answering it, but then thought maybe she wasn't well or something was wrong with the baby, so he pressed the receive button.

"Hello, Jacs. Are you okay?"

"Yes, I am fine, love. I just rang to say Mum asked me if I wanted to stay for dinner as Dad is going to skittles down the *Red Lion* this evening and she'll be on her own. We can both get a chance to catch up on a few episodes of *Call the Midwife*. Are you okay to fix something for yourself?"

Adam felt a flood of relief run through his body.

"Yes, of course. You enjoy yourself. I'll be fine. I'll probably just bang a pizza in the oven."

"Okay. Great. Oh, by the way, did you sort the sink out?"

Adam cursed under his breath.

"Just working on it now when you rang," he lied.

"Oh. Okay. I won't keep you from it. I'll text you later when I'm leaving Mum's."

Adam looked towards the bag longingly, eager to get back to it.

"Okay, love. See you later. Bye."

Adam finished the call and pocketed the phone. He went back to unzipping the bag.

Pulling the zipper all the way, he opened the holdall and took a sharp intake of breath.

Inside was more money than he had ever seen in his life.

All used notes.

He gingerly pulled out a bundle that was held together by an elastic band.

Running his fingers through all, he saw fifties.

Sweet Jesus, how much was in here? Thousands upon thousands. WTF?

Adam suddenly felt scared.

He glanced towards the door, imagining Leon would burst in and confront him.

Used money like this usually meant two things. One, it was stolen or two, it was drugs money or something illegal.

Shit, the sensible thing to do now was to put the bag back and go.

He looked at the cash again.

Yet this money would change Jackie and his lives and also the baby's. They would want for nothing instead of scrimping and saving every fucking penny. They could move to the country. Just disappear. Nobody would know.

Now feeling euphoric, he danced around the room and then stopped, afraid that there may be hidden cameras watching him after all.

He was sweating and his heart was pounding in his chest.

Right, think.

If this was stolen cash or drug money, the owner wasn't going to pop into the local police station and tell them somebody had taken it. No, this was a gift from heaven dropped into Adam's lap.

Whoever left the key in the overcoat fucked up. That wasn't his concern, though.

No, he would take it and sit on it for a while, keep an eye on social media and the news. If nothing was said, then he was home and dry.

What would Jackie say? Her Catholic upbring always gave her a conscience.

He would cross that bridge later.

What if the person who owned this money came here asking for the bag?

Client confidentiality.

If that person didn't have the key and receipt, then they couldn't claim ownership.

Anyway, he was Adam Lucas, not Walter White and he suspected whoever deposited this bag was also not named after the *Breaking Bad* star, so there was no solid proof.

He would be alright. It would work.

He jumped as there was a knock on the door.

"Everything in order, Adam?"

It was Leon.

Adam tried to keep the excitement out of his voice when he replied.

"Yes thanks, Leon. I'm coming out now."

Adam zipped the bag up tightly and unlocked the door.

Leon was waiting outside.

"All good."

Adam nodded.

"Yes, just fine. Thanks, mate. I must dash. I'll give you a call about dinner. Okay?"

Adam came around to the front of the shop and Leon came to the counter and called out to the retreating figure of his friend.

"Take care, mate, and give my love to Jackie."

As Adam left the shop, a man in a dishevelled state who looked as if he was nursing the hangover from hell nearly collided with him.

"Hey. Watch where you're going, buddy," said Adam.

The man barely acknowledged him as he headed towards the *Luggage Safe* desk.

Tommy Scott was on a mission.

Chapter 8

Ronnie Moon had just got off the phone to his sister and the conversation hadn't been pleasant.

A colleague told Ronnie once that he used the phone like a blunt instrument and Ronnie had liked that. He took no prisoners, even if it was Sharon.

Both he and Josie had got back home from visiting Josie's mother about an hour ago.

Ronnie had expected Tommy to be on his way with the bag, but that hadn't happened and he had a bad feeling about it.

He picked up his glass of scotch from the kitchen table and prowled the room like a caged lion.

Josie sat at the island painting her fingernails.

"What did she say?"

Ronnie took a gulp of his drink.

"She is on a break and couldn't talk long, but said she hadn't spoken to Tommy since this morning and that he had been mumbling on about a missing coat and been in a foul mood. Plus, she told me he rolled home in the wee small hours pissed and stoned out of his skull.

That chump has fallen off the wagon and fucked something up. I can sense it. He isn't answering his phone, so I know he is up to no good. I knew I shouldn't have let Sharon talk me into giving him a job. He is a fucking liability.

That bag of cash is a down payment on another important business proposition I have in the pipeline and I need it fast."

He swallowed the rest of his drink and went back to the kitchen table to pour himself another from the bottle standing there.

"What are you going to do, love?" asked Josie as she painted another perfectly manicured nail blood red.

Ronnie looked at her.

"If I don't hear from him in the next couple of hours, then I am doing to pay his house a little visit and see if I can catch the bastard there."

Josie now picked up her gin and tonic.

"Are you one hundred percent sure this geezer delivered the money in the first place from London?"

Ronnie was irritated by the question.

"Of course I fucking am. He wouldn't screw me over. He would be a muppet to try. No, he delivered it and made the key exchange with Tommy. He confirmed that with me."

Josie looked suitably hurt.

"Alright, Ron. I only asked. I'm trying to help."

Ronnie put his glass down and came over to his wife and gently kissed her lips.

"I'm sorry, babes. I didn't mean to shout. Tommy has just wound me up. If he's lost that money, I'll kill the bastard, I swear."

Josie didn't like it when Ronnie got like this. It frightened her.

"Give it another few hours, like you said, and then decide what to do."

Ronnie nodded.

He picked up his drink and headed into the garden.

He needed some fresh air.

Tommy losing the money was bad enough, but what if the little shit had done a runner with it? That was unthinkable.

* * *

Leon Biggs saw the man heading purposely towards the desk. He noticed he was sweating profusely as he got there. Leon could smell alcohol oozing from his pores.

"Yes, can I help you, sir?" asked Leon.

The man got his breath.

"Yes. I deposited a bag here yesterday, but I've mislaid the key."

Leon knew this guy would be trouble. He had a nose for it in this business.

Many a time, things had kicked off in here when circumstances didn't go the way customers planned. Usually when they broke an agreement. Like now.

"Well, that's unfortunate. Have you got the receipt?"

Tommy sighed embarrassingly.

"No, I've lost that also."

"Right. Well, that's not good, I'm afraid," replied Leon.

"Look, mister. I really need your help here. I have to get my bag back."

Leon could see desperation in the man's eyes and felt a pang of empathy.

"I don't suppose you remember the number of the locker you were allocated?"

A light lit up in the man's eyes.

"Yes, I do. Number 79."

"79, you say. Are you sure?"

The man got agitated again.

"Yes, I'm sure. Number 79."

Leon now had a problem as he knew the key Adam had produced had been 79.

There must be some sort of mistake.

"What name was on the receipt, sir?"

Tommy was just about to use his name. Then, he remembered what Joseph Caine had told him.

"Walter White."

Leon tried to hide the surprise from his face.

Key 79 and Walter White were the details Adam had given him. How did this man know them?

"I will just have to go to my office and check the records. I won't be long."

The man nodded.

"Okay, but please hurry. This is urgent."

Once Leon was in his office, he shut the door, pulled out his phone, found Adam's contact number and called it. After a dozen rings, it went to voicemail.

Cursing, Leon left a message:

Adam, ring me as soon as possible. It's urgent. Leon.

He waited a few moments, hoping his friend would get back to him, but nothing. Leon knew he couldn't keep the man waiting at the counter any longer. As he headed back, he thought of what he might say to him.

Suddenly, Leon saw Emily, a fellow member of staff.

"Lisa, you were on duty yesterday, weren't you?"

"Yes, I was. Problem?"

"Do you remember taking in a black holdall for a Walter White and signing it in number 79 locker?"

"Yes, I do. He was the last customer of the day. Why?"

"Would you remember what he looked like?" asked Leon.

Emily nodded.

"Yes, I think so."

Leon guided her by the arm.

"Come with me and discreetly look at the guy standing at the counter and tell me if that is the man from yesterday."

Emily looked at the man from behind the lockers.

She shook her head.

"No. That's not him."

Leon looked suitably pained.

"Are you absolutely sure?"

"Yes, Leon."

"What about the guy that visited me earlier. Did you see him?"

"Sorry, Leon. I was busy. I never noticed him. But if it helps, the guy yesterday who checked in the bag was older, mid-forties probably. Smartly dressed, short grey hair and beard. Well groomed. Reminded me a bit of Bradley Cooper."

Leon sighed.

That was definitely not Adam. This was strange.

"Can you get CCTV footage for yesterday?"

Emily pulled a face.

"Yesterday afternoon the cameras were playing up. We rang a technician, but he couldn't get here until closing time. Henry Gibb, the security guy, stayed with him while he tried to fix the problem, but he needed a special part so he's coming back today. The man you're asking about didn't come in until nearly five."

"So, we have no CCTV in operation?" asked Leon.

Emily shook her head.

"Not since 4.30pm yesterday."

"Why the hell was I not notified?" fumed Leon.

Emily became defensive.

"I put a note in the desk diary on the counter here."

Leon knew he had failed to read the diary entry today.

"Shit," exclaimed Leon, "Okay, Emily, you can go back to work."

Emily walked off, looking confused.

Leon took a deep breath and straightened his tie. He hated these moments and the confrontation which would inevitably follow. How he wished he was at home sat on the sofa with Mo and a large bag of tangy cheese Doritos, drinking Peroni Nastro Azzurro, watching *Squid Games* or *Killing Eve*.

When he returned to the counter, the man was leaning over it impatiently.

"Well, have you found it?"

Leon spoke, trying to keep the slight quiver out of his voice.

"There seems to be a problem, sir. What did you say your name was again?"

"White. Walter White," replied Tommy.

"Did you deposit the bag yesterday yourself?" probed Leon.

This was now getting awkward for Tommy. He couldn't involve Joseph Caine. His job was done.

"No, a friend did."

"Right. And he used your name on the bag?"

Tommy was sweating again.

"Yes. That's right."

"Right. Well, we have two choices here. Either your friend comes back so the member of staff who served him can corroborate that it was him or you can show me some ID to confirm you are who you say you are."

Tommy felt a dread rising in his belly.

"I don't have any with me right now."

Leon heard the hesitation in the man's voice.

"Well, in that case, sir, we have a small problem. If you can return with ID or your friend, then we can see what we can do for you."

Tommy felt the panic rising and his voice rose.

"No, you don't seem to understand. I need my bag right now. I have got to have it NOW."

"I'm sorry, sir. I wouldn't normally be asking for ID, but because you have mislaid the key and..."

Tommy lunged forward and grabbed Leon by the jacket lapels, pulling him up close before he could finish what he was saying. Leon could smell the stale alcohol on the man's breath and also see the menace in his eyes.

"Listen, fat boy. If you don't get me my bag right now, I am going to cause you some fucking damage. Understand?"

Leon held his nerve.

"If you do not let go of me and leave the premises immediately, a colleague is poised and ready to call security and also the police."

For a moment, there was a standoff and then Tommy released his grip.

"I have to inform you, sir, that somebody has already claimed the bag a little earlier," said Leon.

Tommy felt the world around him begin to crumble.

"What the fuck do you mean? How? How did they get it?"

"They came in with the key and receipt. We had no reason to question it."

Tommy steadied himself on the counter.

"I told you, I lost the key and receipt. This fucking muppet must have found it, put two and two together and come in here and you, you fat wanker, just gave them the bag. What was this joker's name?"

"I can't give you that information, I'm afraid," replied Leon.

Tommy lunged at Leon again, but Leon was ready this time and backed away.

"Okay, Emily. Make the call now," he shouted.

Tommy wanted to tear this man apart, but he couldn't risk police involvement.

"You haven't heard the last of this. You will regret what you've done. I'll be back."

He then turned on his heels and stormed off.

Leon breathed a sigh of relief.

"Cup of tea, boss?" asked Emily.

Leon nodded.

"Yes, please. With four sugars."

He headed back to his office. That was enough action for one day.

He suddenly felt peckish and needed another hobnob.

Safely in his office with a steaming mug of tea, Leon thought over what had happened.

Was the bag really this man's? He looked desperate to claim it. If, by some chance, it was, then how did Adam have the key and receipt? The man must be lying. But how did he know the locker number and the name of Walter White? That was too much of a coincidence?

He picked up his phone and called Adam's number again. It went to voicemail.

In frustration, he dropped it back down on his desk.

Something wasn't right here.

Chapter 9

Outside the shop, Tommy kicked out in frustration at an empty Coke can lying on the pavement.

An elderly woman passing by pushing a shopping trolley looked at him disapprovingly.

He ignored her and walked back to his scooter.

He wondered what to do next.

He suddenly realised that his worst nightmare had just come true. This homeless guy who had bought his coat had found the key and had rocked up and took his bag.

Cheeky bastard.

He couldn't ring Ronnie as, by now, he must have concluded that Tommy had fucked up big time.

Tommy couldn't go home.

Ronnie was bound to be on his way down, probably with those two psychos that enforce for him: 'Mad Dog' Marcus Campbell and Ritchie Cummings, aka The Punisher.

Marcus Campbell was eighteen stone of chiselled black muscle. He reminded Tommy of Shadow from the iconic TV programme *Gladiators* that he watched every Saturday night as a teenager back in the day.

Campbell was fucking scary. His eyes were dead like a shark's. He was a black belt in both Karate and Judo. He was lethal with his hands and feet, but also liked to carry a stun gun just for the entertainment of seeing the pain it brought his victims.

Ritchie Cummings was also a right looney tune. Ex-paratrooper. Bald as a snooker ball with a vivid red scar running from his left eye to his chin due to being glassed when he worked on the doors. He was an imposing sight.

The guy who glassed him thought he had got away with it until Ritchie turned up at his mother's house where he was having Sunday dinner. When this geezer opened the front door, Ritchie was standing there wearing a black balaclava. He proceeded to extract a brutal revenge on the man by cutting him a dozen times or more with a razor-sharp Stanley knife. The final act before he left was to cut the victim's left ear clean off. He walked away scot-free after the incident.

The man only survived as his mother had the presence of mind to immediately ring for an ambulance and responded quickly to control the massive blood loss. Since then, in his local neighbourhood, he had become known as 'Jigsaw' because his face was in pieces, or sometimes, he was called 'Twelve Months' as he only had one 'ear.

Ritchie joked about the fact that the man had a missing ear. He told his cronies that he would never be able to wear a pair of glasses again. He had no remorse whatsoever and was gutted the man had survived.

Ritchie did later serve time for smashing up four guys with a sawn-off piece of scaffold bar outside a chip shop one night when they had pushed in front of him in the queue. Miffed at this, Ritchie had gone to the boot of his car and retrieved the scaffold bar. As the four men came out of the chippy tucking into cod, chips and mushy pea, Ritchie set about them like a lunatic. One was left on a life support system for a month before finally recovering. The others had more broken bones than a professional jump jockey.

Up to this point, Ritchie had been staring at a life sentence for murder until the one man finally recovered consciousness. So instead of life, he had done eight years in Wakefield Prison for GBH and wounding with intent, which was no picnic. Wakefield houses some of the most dangerous prisoners in the UK.

Prison did not kerb his violent behaviour. He became known as the 'Punisher' later when he worked for Ronnie because his speciality was torture. He was obsessed with knives.

Tommy felt his sphincter muscle twitch in fear at the thought of these two men getting hold of him.

No. Fuck going home.

He couldn't even tell Sharon. He was too ashamed. Plus, if he did let her in on what had happened, he knew she was terrible at lying and Ronnie would see right through her in seconds. He didn't want to involve her.

He had been a complete idiot and he was now going to have to sort out this mess, which was his own doing.

His only hope was to go back to Gloucester Road and find this homeless bloke.

This sneaky fucker had taken his bag.

He was probably counting out the money now thinking all his Christmas' and birthdays had come in one go. At this moment, he could be planning a round-the-world cruise at Ronnie Moon's expense.

Shit.

Tommy knew he had to track him down. His very life depended on it.

He moved out into the traffic and headed through town and back towards the *Blue Cross* charity shop.

He would ask the woman in the shop he had spoken to earlier more about this bloke who bought his overcoat.

I will find him, thought Tommy.

* * *

The taxi pulled up outside the house and Adam paid the driver and got out clutching the bag.

He had spent his last £20 on the cab fare, but didn't fancy getting on a bus home with the amount of cash in the holdall.

He walked up the driveway to the garage door and opened it.

Looking around to make sure there wasn't any neighbours nosing, he went inside.

Adam now closed down the door and flicked a light switch on. He moved to a work bench in the corner and placed the holdall down on it. He still couldn't believe he had this bag stuffed with money. Mega bucks.

His mobile phone suddenly rang, making him flinch.

Adam read the name of the caller. It was Leon Biggs.

Shit. What did he want?

All sorts of possibilities ran through Adam's head.

Had the owner of the bag turned up demanding it?

Had he demanded Leon to tell him who had taken the bag?

Had Leon grassed him up?

A bang on the garage door nearly had Adam jumping out of his skin.

His heart was banging inside his chest like a triphammer.

Another bang sounded.

Adam instinctively shoved the holdall into a gap between a work bench and an old brown varnished bookcase.

Then, he heard a voice call.

"Adam. Hello. It's Cath from next door. I took a parcel in for Jackie earlier. I have it here."

Adam breathed a sigh of relief.

He moved to the door and opened it, hoping he had some colour back in his face.

Cath Crawley stood outside holding a large, padded jiffy bag.

Adam welcomed her with a smile.

"Thanks, Cath."

She handed him the parcel, glancing over his shoulder to see what he was up to in the garage.

Cath was in her fifties with a pleasant face, but she could have benefitted from losing a few stone. Her husband, Bill, who was a long-distance lorry driver, was also bordering on being obese, no doubt as a result of his network of greasy spoon truck stops across the country and Cath's cooking.

She especially loved her baking and was always bringing Adam and Jackie some of her homemade offerings. Her fruit scones and coffee and walnut cake were to die for.

"You're welcome, love. Sorry to pounce on you as soon as you got home, but I have to go out. Dental appointment," she explained.

"No worries, Cath. And thanks once again."

Cath stole another glance into the garage and then waddled off. Adam shut down the door again.

He chuckled to himself.

It had only been Cath Crawley, not some hitman or mafia gangster after his blood.

She was definitely nosy and a gossip, but not a killer.

His phone rang again.

It was Leon.

He decided to take it. He couldn't avoid him forever.

Adam answered, sounding cheery and relaxed.

"Hi, Leon. What's up?"

Leon's voice was low, and it sounded strained.

"Thank fuck you answered. I've tried you umpteen times."

"I was in a cab, mate. What's the matter?"

"The matter is not long after you left with your bag, a geezer came in here looking for it. He told me he had mislaid the key and receipt, but he knew the number on the key and that the name was Walter White.

When I explained that somebody had already claimed the bag, he was not a happy bunny. I mean, if looks could kill... I had to threaten him with the police to get him to leave. But he said he would come back. What the fuck is going on here, Adam?"

Adam could now hear the anger rising in his friend's voice.

"Look, Leon. I don't know anything about this bloke or how he knew the name on the ticket. Maybe he is just some chancer that was stood behind me when I checked the bag in. That is probably..."

"Fucking stop there, Adam!" shouted Leon.

Adam was taken back by the venom in his retort.

"One of my trusted staff remember the bag being checked in and her description of the man who checked it in doesn't fit this geezer who was after it and it doesn't fit you either. So, cut the bullshit and tell me what is going on here; otherwise, I will have to get the police involved and I really don't want to do that."

Adam knew he had to level with Leon.

He admitted that the bag wasn't his. He then went on to tell Leon what was in the bag.

Leon was stunned.

"How much money exactly is in this bag?"

"I haven't had time to count it, but it is a fucking lot. Possibly a quarter of a million, maybe more."

"Shit, Adam. You know this money is from something heavy, probably drugs. This bloke who came in for the bag isn't just going to walk away from it. He'll be back. In my opinion, he's just the organ grinder doing his job, but I don't want the fucking monkey turning up here. I have got a feeling in my water that he will be an evil bastard. Nobody wants to lose a quarter of a million quid.

Get that bag back here right now and I will smooth things over with this guy when he returns, and nobody will be any the wiser."

"Hey, wait a second, my friend. This is a lifechanging sum of money we're talking about. I'm prepared to cut you in on the deal. If this money is iffy, then this bloke isn't going to involve the coppers or any authority, is he? What can he do?"

"That may be true, but he could come back here mob handed and break my fucking legs," replied Leon.

Adam laughed.

"A wedge of this money should ease the pain."

"Very funny, Adam."

"Mate, you didn't personally know anything about the bag. If I had waltzed in with the key and you didn't know me, you still would have given me the bag. You weren't to know, so you are in the clear. As far as you are concerned, this Walter White collected as normal. Right?"

"Well ,when you look at it like that, I suppose you're right. But still..."

Leon was wavering.

Adam carried on.

"Look, Leon. You've told me for years now that you would love to go on a world cruise. First class all the way. Champagne. Captain's table. Isn't it your 40th coming up soon? Well, here is your chance. Maureen would fucking love it too. You would be a proper solid gold hero. Think about it."

There was silence on the end of the phone.

"What about the San Diego comic con? The tickets are like gold dust, but you would have no problem getting hold of them."

He knew to attend the legendary comic con was on Leon's bucket list.

"Also, my friend, the icing on the cake is the Marvel Silver Age comic Avengers number 1. The superhero holy grail, my friend."

Leon's heart beat faster.

Every Marvel comic collector wanted that rare copy in their collection. It was fetching a price between £3,000 and £3,500.

"Listen, Leon. Jacs is at her mum's until later. Come around to mine straight after you finish work and let's talk about this properly. Let's not do anything rash or something that we will regret. Okay?"

Adam held his breath and crossed his fingers as he waited for his friend to reply.

Finally, Leon spoke.

"I'll be there at 7.00pm.But this doesn't mean I agree to anything. Understand?"

"I understand. See you then."

Adam disconnected the call.

He pulled the holdall out of its hiding place and brought it to the work bench.

Unzipping it, he emptied out all the contents and began to count the money.

It took some time.

When he had finished, it came to £350,000.

Adam stood back from the bench and looked at the piles of cash.

He knew the money would help to get a better house in a decent area for the arrival of the baby and also pay off the debts they had accumulated on their credit cards.

Who knows what else?

That trip to Paris that was at present a pipe dream or a new and reliable family car?

He felt butterflies fluttering in his stomach at the prospect of a better life for Jackie and himself.

Fuck it, he could put this dirty money to some good. Whoever it belonged to probably had loads more. They would get over it.

All he had to do was sit on it for a while and remain anonymous.

There was no way he could be found.

He would deal with Jackie later. For now, it was Leon who he had to win around.

Chapter 10

Sharon Scott rang her husband's mobile and, once more, it went to answerphone. Five minutes ago, she had spoken to Ronnie on the phone, and he told her he was getting ready to head down to Bristol to have a word, as he put it, with Tommy.

Sharon had explained to her brother that she hadn't heard from Tommy since this morning as she had then been working at the hospital.

She was now on a cigarette break and told Ronnie to give her half an hour to see if she could contact her husband before he made the journey.

Ronnie was not a happy man, but agreed to give her thirty minutes. He concluded the conversation by telling her if he didn't hear back from her, he was coming.

Sharon was in a panic. What had Tommy done? Whatever it was, Ronnie was fuming and she feared for her husband's wellbeing.

She had seen Ronnie extract revenge on a few people in the past and it was not a pretty sight.

She rang Tommy's phone again and when it went to voicemail, she left a message.

Tommy, ring me. I don't know what's happened and I don't care. Just ring me. You have Ronnie breathing down your neck. I have stalled him from coming down here, but it won't be for long unless you contact him now.

Sharon finished the call and chewed her nails, hoping her phone would ring soon.

She glanced at the clock. She had twenty minutes left.

* * *

Tommy parked the scooter outside the charity shop. As he did so, his phone rang. He checked the screen. It was Sharon. He couldn't answer it. The less she knew, the better. He pocketed the phone as he heard it ping a voicemail.

He entered the shop. It was empty, except for the woman behind the counter that he had spoken to earlier.

Tommy moved to the counter.

"Excuse me, I was in earlier about my overcoat that got sold by mistake. Do you remember me?"

Pat Hargreaves' eyes narrowed.

"Yes, I do recall, but I'm afraid it hasn't been returned, nor any of its contents."

Tommy nodded.

"Okay, thank you. Can I ask… could you describe for me again the man who bought it? He's a homeless guy who hangs around the street here, so your colleague told me."

"Yes, apparently so, but I don't know much about him. Jean is the one you need to speak to."

"Right. Can I speak to her then?"

"I'm afraid she's not here at present."

"When will she be back?"

"Not for a week. She's gone on holiday."

"Shit," Tommy blurted out.

"I beg your pardon?" replied Pat.

"Sorry. It's just that this is urgent, and I really need to talk to her."

Tommy was doing his best to hold his temper.

"Well, she won't be in until next Monday."

Tommy groaned in desperation.

"Is there not anything you can remember about him?"

"I didn't really pay much attention and, to be honest, one homeless person looks like another to me. Sorry."

Tommy knew he was done here.

Outside the shop, he checked his phone and listened to the voicemail from Sharon. A tremor of fear ran through his body.

Ronnie was on his way, and he didn't have his money. He was a dead man once those two lunatics, Campbell and Cummings, got at him.

Shit. What was he going to do?

He had to somehow buy himself some time.

Tommy decided to ring Sharon.

She picked it up on the first ring.

"Thank God, Tommy. Are you alright? I am at my wit's end. Ronnie is coming. What have you done?"

She was babbling and Tommy had to cut her short.

"Listen carefully to me, Sharon. I have got myself in a bit of a jam. I am not going into the details now."

Sharon attempted to speak, but Tommy ploughed on.

"I need a few days to sort things, so I'm not coming home, neither am I facing your Ronnie at this moment in time to explain myself; otherwise, I suspect you will be paying me daily visits in intensive care."

Sharon began to sob.

"When Ronnie asks you about me, tell him that you have heard nothing from me and my phone keeps going to voicemail. Tell him you're scared that I may have had an accident or gone on a drugs and booze bender. I am going to try and kip down at a mate's tonight and then hopefully sort this mess out tomorrow. Until then, just keep schtum and say nothing. Do you understand?"

"What happened, Tommy? Please tell me," pleaded Sharon.

"Do you understand what I've just said? The less you know the better when that brother of yours starts turning up the heat. I will be in touch again soon. I promise."

Tommy cut the call.

He decided he would go and find Finlay and bed down on his sofa.

* * *

The thirty minutes had come and gone, and Sharon had not phoned back.

Ronnie Moon now sat in the passenger seat of the black Mercedes. Across from him driving the car was Marcus Campbell. He was the picture of concentration as he navigated the small Cotswolds lanes heading out towards the bigger A-roads and then the motorway down to Bristol.

In the back seat was Ritchie Cummings. He was reading a dog-eared paperback copy of *Pretty Boy*, the autobiography of the late Roy Shaw who had been a property investor, author and businessman from the East End of London who was formerly a criminal, Category A prisoner and a ferocious unlicensed boxer and streetfighter.

He was probably best remembered for his three unlicensed boxing matches with another legendary fighter and 'Guvnor', Lenny McLean.

Ronnie looked out the window deep in thought. He wondered what had happened to the money. Tommy wouldn't be stupid enough to do a runner with it, would he?

No, he wouldn't leave Sharon behind. Unless she was in on it?

Fuck, no way. He had offered Sharon thousands over the years, and she wouldn't take it, so she wasn't likely to steal his money.

So, what the fuck happened and where was Tommy?

Had somebody mugged him over for the bag?

Or had Joseph Caine and his boss really double crossed him and stolen the money back after all?

He felt a headache coming. There were too many unanswered questions for his liking.

Tommy Scott needed to answer those questions and how he answered them would decide his fate.

The three men were all carrying firearms only to be used as a last resort. All the guns were unmarked and untraceable.

Funny how staring down the barrel of a Glock 17 can be a religious experience and instantly jog the memory of some uncooperating punter.

The Mercedes they were driving had false plates on.

This unscheduled visit to Bristol would be done under the radar.

It was not often these days that Ronnie had to dirty his hands with this sort of thing, but he took this little episode personally.

He looked at his watch

Another thirty minutes or so should find him in Bristol.

He would track down Tommy, even if it took him all night.

Yes, he would find the little bastard, no matter where he was holed up.

* * *

Leon Biggs stood on the porch step and rang the doorbell. The door was almost instantly opened by Adam.

"Come in, Leon. Thanks for coming over."

Adam ushered his friend inside and shut the door.

"Come in through to the living room. Can I get you a beer? I've just opened one."

"Yeah, I'll have one. I feel I have earnt it today."

Adam laughed nervously.

"Right, yeah. Take a seat and I'll get one. San Miguel alright?"

"Sure," replied Leon.

Adam disappeared into the kitchen and returned moments later with an ice-cold beer and handed it to Leon.

"There you go, buddy."

He clinked his bottle with Leon's and sat down in an armchair facing his friend who sat on the sofa.

Leon took a long pull on his beer and then looked at Adam.

"Right then, spill the fucking beans, and it better be good."

Over the next fifteen minutes, Adam told Leon the lot.

How he was working on the streets for his proposed book, bought the overcoat because he was freezing, found the key in the pocket's lining and turned up at *Luggage Safe*. Then, he told him about the money he found in the holdall.

"£350K,you say," exclaimed Leon, eyes wide in utter disbelief.

Adam smiled.

"Yep. All in used, and I suspect, untraceable notes. It's a fucking dream find. We would be fools to hand it in."

"That may be so, but the guy who claims it is his told me he would come back and I don't think he is coming back to deliver me flowers," replied Leon, "He could firebomb the shop or open up with a shooter. He might even wait for me after I lock up and stab me to death. Fuck knows what he's capable of doing or the person I suspect he is working for.

"Listen Leon. Don't fucking panic. As I said previously, that guy is fucked .He was using your storage shop to hide illegal money. Drug money probably. He has lost it. You just done your job. Nothing more or nothing less. You can't take responsibility for this joker losing his key.

People use your place because it is discreet, and no questions are asked. No names are checked, and no ID required; just the key and the receipt. Nobody can be traced once they pick up their bag and go. This guy is probably up to his neck in shit to whoever he works for and he isn't going to involve the police. I am telling you, he's screwed. There's nothing he can do. We sit on the money for a while until it all dies down and goes away and then Bob's you uncle. We're rich."

Leon took another pull on his beer and swallowed deeply.

"I don't know, Adam. This is madness."

Adam leaned forward in his chair.

"Of course it's madness, but you only get one opportunity in this life. Let's take it. I clear my debt and start fresh, and you treat yourself to the holiday of a lifetime. First class all the way. You get to the comic con. Christ, Leon, you deserve it. As long as I have known you, you have worked your balls off in mundane 9 to 5 jobs. You deserve better."

Leon drained his bottle.

"Get me another and let's look at this properly, shall we?

Adam grinned and got up from his chair.

"Sure thing, buddy. Let's get another beer and I will show you the money."

Five minutes later, both men stood in the garage with the money laid out on the work bench.

"Sweet Jesus. I have never seen so much cash," exclaimed Leon.

He picked up a bundle in his chubby paw and smelt it, then ran his fingers through it.

He was seduced.

"Right. This bag needs to be stored safely for a good few months. We can't risk anybody seeing us spending large sums of cash. I would normally suggest *Luggage Safe*, but not on this occasion. That would be far too risky. This guy who claims the bag is his will probably be watching me closely. Also, we don't meet up and only text each other when necessary."

Adam nodded.

"Is the bag safe here for now?" asked Leon.

"Yes. Nobody except you knows I have it. It will be perfectly safe."

Leon nodded.

"Good. I could store it at *Luggage Safe*, but as I already said, it might prove too risky if anybody comes sniffing around."

"Okay. So, we agree that we are keeping it. Yes?" asked Adam.

Leon's face broke into a big cheesy grin.

"Yes. Fuck it. We keep it."

"In that case..." said Adam.

He peeled off a handful of notes for each of them from a bundle.

"We use this for a discreet celebration in lieu of the big landslide to come."

Both men clinked bottles together and pocketed the cash.

Adam returned the rest of the cash to the bag and then hid the holdall at the back of the work bench behind other boxes, bags and camping gear.

For now, it was safe.

"Listen, Adam," said Leon, "As great as a bunch of cash is in this day and age, how the fuck can you use it without drawing suspicion to yourself? You can't exactly deposit in the bank, can you?"

Adam frowned. He hadn't thought of that.

"Look, we'll cross that bridge when the time arrives. I have an uncle who has done time in the past. He was a bit of a crook in his day. Frank is the black sheep of the family, and nobody really talks about him. I'm sure he'll know how to sort the money out for a fee. For now, let's just agree we are going to keep it. Okay?"

Leon smiled and nodded.

"Let's celebrate with one more beer before the Mrs gets back," said Adam.

* * *

Later that night as Adam lay in bed listening to Jackie's gentle snoring next to him, thoughts of sleep were the last thing on his mind. He kept seeing, in his mind's eye, the bag of cash and he kept thinking about what he could do with it. He was 99% sure that there was no comeback to him.

For now, the money was safe. He would say nothing to Jackie about it until need be. He didn't want anything to jeopardise the birth of their baby and he didn't want Jackie upset.

He would take her out for a meal tomorrow evening on the money he had skimmed from the bag, but tell her that he had come up trumps on a scratch card.

Come Monday morning, he would be back on the streets acting as normal so that Jackie would not get suspicious.

He still wanted to write the book regardless. To prove he could.

By the time she had arrived home earlier that evening, Leon was gone. The empties were in the recycling, and he had sorted the sink out. So, all was good. He just had to keep his nerve and he hoped Leon would as well.

Chapter 11

As suspected, Tommy found Finlay in the *Green Man* on the pool table. He waited until he had finished his game and then caught his eye.

They moved to a corner table.

"Tommy, I didn't expect to see you again so soon. I can't believe Sharon let you out after last night's debauchery."

"She hasn't. I was hoping to kip down at yours for the night."

Finlay smiled.

"Yeah, no problem. What's up then?"

"I'm in deep fucking shit. That's what is up."

Over a few beers, Tommy explained the whole sorry situation and how he had fucked up the job he was doing yesterday and at present couldn't go home as Sharon's brother was after his balls.

"This is some shit storm you have walked into, my friend. But exactly how bad is it?" said Finlay.

"Believe me, it's bad. A lot of money is involved and that makes things dangerous."

Finlay could see his friend was worried.

"Can I help in any way?"

Tommy swallowed a mouthful of beer as a thought came to his head.

Finlay was streetwise and knew a who's who of faces out there. Just maybe...

Tommy took a gamble.

"I need to find a homeless guy who has recently started hanging out on Gloucester Road. I believe he bought my coat and found the key."

"Right. Then in that case, we need to go and see Rat," replied Finlay.

"Rat? Who the hell is Rat when he's at home."

Finlay laughed.

"That's just it. He is not at home, any home. He is king of the streets here in Bristol. He knows everybody in the area living rough. He will find this dude. I guarantee it."

"Right. Where do we find him?"

"Hold your horses, cowboy. We need to grease his palms, so to speak."

Tommy finished off his beer.

"You mean money?"

"Hopefully not. I'm betting on twenty Lambert and Butler and four cans of Carlsberg special brew should do it."

Ten minutes later, they came out of *Patel's* corner shop with their purchases.

"Okay, where do we find this Rat character?" asked Tommy.

"On a weekend night, he will most likely be in the town centre looking to hit on a few affluent punters coming out of a show or a bar."

"Right, hop on the back end of the scooter and hold onto me tight. We're going to take a ride."

Finlay eyed the scooter nervously.

"The two of us won't fit onto that, I'm sure."

"We'll fucking have to, my son. Come on. Let's go."

* * *

Sharon soaked in the bath with her CD of dolphin sounds playing in the background. She sipped on a glass of chardonnay and tried to relax in the aftermath of Ronnie's visitation.

He had arrived like a lion along with two right bruisers, but had gone out like a lamb eventually after he had vented his anger.

He had told her the full story of the job that had been assigned to Tommy, how he had to retrieve a key and then pick up the bag from the locker. A bag containing a lot of money.

Sharon began to piece together in her head what might have happened.

Ronnie hadn't gone completely. He was driving around some of the local hospitals to check if a Tommy Scott had been brought in after Sharon had convinced him that her husband might actually be injured or ill.

Ronnie had tried to rationalise what Sharon had told him and maybe – just maybe – the stupid prat had been involved in an accident of some sort and couldn't get to a phone.

There was a distant possibility that maybe he hadn't fucked up and lost his money.

Seeing the state his sister was in, he was prepared to give her husband the benefit of the doubt for now.

He told Sharon to have a bath and a glass of wine and try to relax.

Ronnie assured her if he found Tommy, he would allow him to tell his story first.

As he opened the front door, he told her that he would bring back a takeaway when he had finished.

When he left the house, she breathed a sigh of relief. Once more, she had managed to get Tommy a brief reprieve. She hoped it would be enough to help him out.

Ronnie had made it clear that if he had fucked up the job, the two gorillas with him were going to put the hurt on Tommy big time. She couldn't let that happen.

Whatever Tommy had done, she still loved him unconditionally. She would do whatever it took to keep him safe., even if it meant going up against her psycho brother.

* * *

"Where the fuck is this guy, Fin? This scooter is costing me a fortune with money I don't have to spend. When Sharon sees the bank account, she'll kill me," shouted Tommy above the noise of the traffic.

"He'll be here somewhere. Go around the one-way system again, will you? But slower this time," replied Finlay.

On the way back around, Finlay shouted out and pointed.

"There he is over by the waterfront by that doughnut stall."

Tommy swung the scooter left and come up on the pavement, then across onto the cobbles by the dockside.

The area was teaming with people drinking and eating from the many takeaway stalls along the front. Music played and everybody was in a good weekend mood.

Finlay headed towards a man sat on a blanket eating an iced doughnut with a scruffy looking mongrel lying next to him sleeping.

Tommy followed, pushing his scooter.

As he got closer, he observed Rat.

He was probably in his early forties. Tall and gangly. Not an ounce of fat on him. He had a sort of pirate look about him like Johnny Depp from the movies.

Rat wore multiple layers of clothing of all styles and colours to keep out the bitter November chill. He also sported on his head one of those woollen caps with the ear flaps.

Finlay had told Tommy on the journey to the city centre that Rat's real name was Joshua Candy. Ex-university dropout who backpacked around the world on Daddy's money, spending it like water until it ran out and Daddy kicked him out of the family home and any inheritance. He took to the streets and had been there ever since. He was one of life's survivors.

Rat had become a bit of a sage among the homeless. He was always available with good advice, spiritual guidance or words of wisdom to those who found themselves without a roof over their heads.

He had lived on the streets of Bristol for fifteen years and knew them inside out. The nickname Rat had come about because of his uncanny capacity to find free food wherever he was. His reputation was phenomenal.

Rat had just played half an hour on an old battered acoustic guitar that had attracted a crowd, many of whom bought doughnuts from the stall he sat by. When he had finished playing, as a way of thanks for boosting his profits, the owner of the *Doughnut Den* gave Rat a bag of assorted goodies to eat.

"Hey, Rat. Been a while. How are you, man?" asked Finlay.

Rat looked up from devouring his doughnut and his weathered features broke into a grin, revealing a row of surprisingly even white teeth.

"Fin, it has been an age. What brings you down here?"

"Rat, let me introduce you to a very good friend of mine, Tomo."

Tommy came forward.

"Hello. Nice to meet you."

Rat studied him for a moment and then nodded.

"Nice to meet you also, Tomo. Any friend of Fin and all that."

Tommy smiled.

"How do you guys know each other?"

Fin looked at Rat and then to Tommy.

"Well, going back a fair few years ago, my landlord evicted me from my flat as he found out I was growing cannabis in there. He didn't want to involve the police so he told me he would not contact them if I left and he could keep the plants.

Well, he had me between a rock and a hard place, so I left my home and also my income. For a while, I took to living on the streets and on my very first night, I met Rat and he took me under his wing, so to speak, and showed me the ropes. I lived for a year homeless and wouldn't have survived without this man's help."

Rat held up his hands in mock surrender.

"You overexaggerate my help. It was nothing really."

Finlay smiled.

"You are too modest, my friend. I will never forget your mentoring."

Rat seemed embarrassed and changed the subject .

"Anyway, as I asked, what brings you here?"

"We need your help on an urgent matter," answered Finlay.

Rat raised his eyebrows.

"I'm intrigued. Come and join me on my blanket. It's quite safe. I have a friend, Cherie, who works at the local launderette. She washes it for me free of charge, of course, whenever the boss isn't around."

He gestured to the dog.

"Don't mind Bojo there. He is docile."

As the two men sat down, Rat eyed the plastic bag hooked onto the scooter handle bars.

"Is that for me by any chance?"

Tommy reached up and got it.

"Yes, it is. Just a few things for your time."

Rat looked inside and smiled. He pulled out a can of lager, cracked it open, took a long swig and then belched.

"Why, thank you, boys. Now how can I help?"

Finlay let Tommy explain about the homeless man they were looking for. Tommy didn't explain exactly why they were looking for him and Rat didn't ask.

Rat listened while he finished off his can and then spoke.

"You said he wore a Spiderman beanie. Is that right?"

"Yes, that's right. Do you know him?" asked Tommy with some urgency in his voice.

This didn't go unnoticed by Rat.

"I have seen him around the last month or so. Mainly along Gloucester Road. He usually sits outside *McDonald's*. I spoke to him briefly a few weeks back.

I introduced myself and told him a few ground rules to adhere to. He thanked me and then went on his way.

I then bumped into him again last week. We shared a coffee in the Memorial Park under the shelter there. He was a nice guy so I had time for him. I told him my background and status on the streets. He was really interested. He then surprised me by telling me that he wasn't actually homeless at all."

Tommy and Finlay exchanged glances.

"What do you mean?" asked Tommy.

Rat opened another can.

"He confided in me that he was a writer and he was going to write a novel centred around a homeless person. He was living on the streets on and off to do background research. He went home every night. His name is Adam, I recall. He told me he would love to talk to me again as he could build the book's character around me. I was flattered, to say the least. He then slipped me a twenty for my trouble and went on his way."

Tommy felt hope rising inside him, but tried not to show his excitement.

"Do you know where he went or where he really lives?"

Rat shook his head.

"No. He didn't tell me anything more private about himself."

"Shit," exclaimed Tommy.

The hope he felt a moment ago was beginning to diminish.

Rat saw the look of deflation on Tommy's face.

"Is it really important to you to find this man?" asked Rat.

"Yes, it is really important. If you can find him again, there's fifty quid in it for you."

"Fifty quid. Well, fuck me. Why didn't you say so? I can definitely find him for you."

"You can?" asked Tommy.

"How can you be so sure, Rat?" said Finlay.

"Because before he left me, we agreed to meet again this Monday, tomorrow in the Memorial Park at 11.00am to talk about more stuff for his book. He also promised me another twenty quid."

"Fucking hell, Rat. You have just come up trumps!" exclaimed Tommy as he clapped the man on the shoulder.

Finlay's face broke into a huge grin.

"I told you Rat would help us, didn't I?"

Both men high fived.

"Rat, you don't know what this means to me. Seriously."

Rat raised his can.

"Happy to help. But I will take that fifty in advance if you don't mind."

For a moment, Tommy hesitated.

Would this guy just fuck off with his money never to be seen again?

Then he also didn't want to insult him.

"So, let me clarify your meet again."

"Tomorrow morning at 11.00am in the shelter inside Hawthorne Memorial Park. Gloucester Road," repeated Rat.

Tommy nodded.

"Okay, where is the nearest cash point?"

Rat told them where to go and said he would be here waiting for them.

Before they left, Rat asked.

"You aren't going to hurt this guy, are you? I am against any violence, and I wouldn't want to be jeopardising him in any way."

"No. It's nothing like that. Just a bit of business. That's all. Nothing heavy," replied Tommy.

As Rat watched the two men disappear, he wondered what they really wanted with this Adam guy. Business bollocks. That was a lie. By the look on this Tomo's face, he was desperate to find him.

Maybe there might be an angle to work here to get old Rat a few more quid.

Chapter 12

Ronnie returned to Sharon's just after 11.30pm armed with a Chinese takeaway. Sharon wasn't really hungry, but she didn't want to upset Ronnie any more than necessary, so she accepted the sweet and sour pork.

His two cronies had booked into a Travelodge nearby. She was grateful for that fact, as she didn't want them in her house. They radiated violence.

As Sharon busied herself getting some cutlery, her brother poured himself a glass of wine.

"I went around the main hospitals, but there's no evidence that Tommy has been in them. So, we can pretty much write off the accident theory."

"Maybe he's in police custody instead. If he is back on the gear, God knows what he might get up to?" said Sharon, hoping that Ronnie may consider this option.

He came out into the kitchen and stood in the doorway.

"Yeah, it's a possibility, I suppose, but if that is the case, I won't just be able to waltz into a nick and ask, will I?"

Sharon said nothing.

Ronnie continued.

"I partly blame you for this mess, Sharon. You pestered me to give Tommy a job against my better instincts and now look what's happened."

"Well, maybe you shouldn't have trusted him with such an important pick up and used somebody more experienced,' retorted Sharon.

Ronnie swallowed the rest of his drink and slammed the glass down on a worktop.

"Don't smart-mouth me, lady. The job was sound, and he was well capable of completing t. Only, I suspect, he got coerced somehow into drinking and drugs again. There is a fucking lot of money missing and Tommy knows about it and is not answering his phone. I want to know where my bag is. I don't give two fucks about the waster. I just want what is mine."

Ronnie looked Sharon straight in the eye.

"Are you sure he hasn't been in touch with you?"

There was menace in his voice that Sharon didn't like.

Although Sharon was frightened, she spoke sharply.

"Listen here, Ronnie. You don't just walk into my house and start laying the law down. Also, you don't talk to me like one of your thugs. I am your sister. Have some respect. I have told you I don't know where Tommy is. You may only care about your money, but he's my husband and I am worried sick that he has not come home. For all we know, he could be dead in a ditch somewhere."

Ronnie was silent for a moment. Then, he walked across to his sister.

"I'm sorry. You're right. I shouldn't take it out on you. It's been a long day. Come on. Let's eat and then get some rest."

He put his arm around Sharon. They walked back into the living room.

As they entered the room, Sharon's mobile, which was on the arm of the sofa, went off.

She froze as her ringtone of Ed Sheeran's 'Shape of You' sounded over and over.

"Well, aren't you going to answer it?" asked Ronnie.

Sharon's heart sunk as she walked across to the phone and saw Tommy's name on the screen.

As she went to pick it up, the phone stopped ringing.

She inwardly said a thank you to God.

"Who was it?" asked Ronnie.

"Just a miscall. I didn't recognise the number."

Sharon prayed that he would let it go.

"Bit late for a miscall, isn't it?" pursued Ronnie.

Sharon laughed nervously.

"Yeah. Well, never mind. Let's eat this food before it goes cold, shall we?

Ronnie nodded.

Suddenly, the phone blipped with an answerphone message.

"Better see who that is, Sharon," said Ronnie.

"Let's eat first."

Ronnie walked up to Sharon and before she could react, he took the phone from her hand and pressed the voicemail, putting it on loudspeaker.

Sharon slumped to the sofa as Tommy's voice came on.

Hi Sharon, it's me. I know I'm taking a chance, but I had to tell you. I've had a break. I think I've located the geezer who bought my coat. I'll explain why that is so important later. I can't get to him until tomorrow, but I'm sure I can sort things out and resolve the situation. Is that maniac brother of yours in Bristol yet? If so, please try and stall him. I'm staying at Finlay Bryant's gaff for a few nights in Stokes Croft. I'll let you know when I get things sorted out. Take care.

I love you. Everything is gonna be alright. I promise.
Just stall Ronnie.

The call cut off.

Ronnie pocketed the phone.

"Well, well, well. Good old Tommy is alive and well after all. Seems like he has lost my money and you know something about it. Time to spill the beans and I just might let him live."

Sharon sighed in resignation.

She told her brother about how Tommy had come home in the small hours out of his skull and how they had rowed. Then she mentioned the mix-up with the coat and the charity shop and how Tommy had gone mad and panicked when he knew the coat was gone.

Ronnie listened.

From what Sharon had told him and the voicemail, it looked like the key to the locker with his money in it had been in the coat and somebody inadvertently bought it from the charity shop that it mistakenly ended up in.

The question was, did that person find it? And if so, did they work out what the key was for?

Only Tommy could answer those questions and they needed to be answered now.

"This Finlay character Tommy mentioned, where in Stokes Croft does he live?"

Ronnie looked his sister in the eye.

"Please don't try to bullshit me, Sharon. The time for games are over."

Sharon sighed in resignation and sat forward on the sofa.

"If it's the same place he's always lived in, I would have his number in the phone address book."

She went to the hallway and retrieved it from a small table by the front door.

Bringing it back into the living room, she thumbed through it.

"Here it is. Number 42 Herald Way, a couple of doors down from the *Turk's Head* pub. But that was a few years back he lived there. I didn't even realise that both of them were back together again. Finlay was a bad influence on Tommy, and they parted company a long time ago."

"Well, it looks like they're buddies once more. I don't suppose this Finlay might persuade your husband to take my money, do you?"

"Christ no, Ronnie. Tommy can be an idiot sometimes, but he wouldn't do that. No way."

Ronnie pulled out his phone.

"You better hope for Tommy's sake that is the case."

Ronnie hit a number and the call was answered almost immediately.

"Marcus, you and Ritchie get yourselves ready. I will pick you up in ten minutes. We have a little late night house call to make."

Ronnie pocketed his phone and headed for the door. He looked back at his sister.

"I'm sorry the little shit has fucked up. He's let us both down. I cannot and will not let that go. Do you understand?"

Sharon sat there numbly and nodded her head.

"He said he could get the money back. Give him a chance and let him try; otherwise, if you hurt him, you may never get it back, will you?

Ronnie regarded his sister. There was some truth in what she said.

"I will see what he's got to say for himself first. So, no promises. He's fucked up and has to pay somehow. That is just the way it is."

"Ronnie, God knows how you're my brother. You're an evil bastard underneath your successful businessman exterior. A fucking monster."

Ronnie smiled.

"You've known that for years, Sharon, but it didn't stop you coming to me to give your husband a job, did it? Don't fucking judge me, sis. Take a look at yourself instead. If you choose to swim in shark-infested water, don't be surprised that you just might get bitten."

With that, he left the room and Sharon heard the front door close. A few minutes later, she heard Ronnie's car start. She went to the window to make sure he had gone.

She didn't give a damn what Ronnie had said. She needed to warn her husband before it was too late. She ran to the sideboard, opened the top drawer and rifled through it until she found an old pay-as-you-go phone and a charger. She prayed it would work.

***

After giving Rat his money, Tommy and Finlay headed back to Stokes Croft on the scooter. They pulled into Herald Way and Finlay saw the lights of the *Turk's Head* still on.

"Looks like old Eddie, the landlord, is having one of his infamous Sunday night lock-ins. Shall we celebrate our recent good fortune with a few beers?" said Finlay.

"Okay," replied Tommy, "I'm just going to give Sharon a quick call."

Finlay nodded and wandered off a short distance to light up a cigarette and wait.

Tommy noticed his phone's battery was on ten percent. He needed to charge it soon.

He made the call, but got Sharon's answerphone. He left her a voicemail message.

He felt bad now about shouting at her earlier. If he had done the job properly in the first place, then the coat going to the charity shop wouldn't have mattered.

She couldn't have known. She had always been nothing, but 100% supportive of him over the years. He had been a fool to kick off.

His blistering hangover this morning hadn't give him any room for empathy or reason. Now sober, he realised what a dick he had been. He hoped and prayed that, come Monday, he would have sorted out this mess. If he could get the money back, maybe – just maybe – he might be spared Ronnie Moon's wrath.

* * *

The Jaguar silently pulled up across the road from 42 Herald Way. Inside the car, Ronnie Moon looked at the miscall from Tommy on Sharon's phone and smiled to himself.

"Here we are, boys. Time for a little house call."

Marcus Campbell and Ritchie Cummings both nodded in unison.

The house was in darkness.

"Right, Marcus. Let Ritchie and me out and you park up around the corner and then check to see if there is a back entrance to this dump."

"Will do, boss," replied Marcus.

The two men exited the car and watched it disappear around the corner.

They now both slipped on surgical gloves.

They crossed the road and walked up to the shabby grey front door. It hadn't seen a lick of paint for some time.

"Here we go then," said Ronnie.

Ritchie rang the doorbell.

Both men waited.

Nothing.

"Try it again," said Ronnie.

* * *

Inside the *Turk's Head* was around a dozen or so people all happily enjoying the unofficial extended drinking hours, trying to put off the thought of work later that day for another few hours.

Finlay and Tommy were on their third scotch.

Finlay rifled through his pockets.

"What the fuck are you looking for?" asked Tommy.

Finlay grinned.

"I thought I had some weed on me, but it must be at home. I could murder a joint."

Tommy nodded as he finished his scotch.

Finlay stood up.

"Get another round in and I'll pop back to the house and grab a couple. The night is young, my friend."

Tommy watched his friend stagger slightly and then head towards the side door.

He then stopped and had a word with the red-haired girl he had introduced to him earlier.

She was a mate and a neighbour. Lisa Miller.

Tommy saw the girl pass Fin some money and he slipped it into his jeans pocket, nodded and left the pub.

Tommy got up and went to the bar.

As he waited to be served, he felt in a more relaxed mood. No doubt the Famous Grouse was helping. He was optimistic that, come tomorrow, he would have the money back.

If things got heavy with this guy who took it, he would have to take things up a notch. He realised this.

Although he wasn't a violent man, he could be if necessary.

Yes, if he had to fuck this thieving little bastard up, he was ready to do so.

The situation had now become dog eat dog and he hoped he had the bigger teeth.

Tommy collected the drinks and headed back to his seat.

* * *

After ringing the doorbell half a dozen times, Ronnie contemplated his next move. Maybe Marcus might have found a way in around the back.

"Let's try the back way," he informed Ritchie.

As the two men walked off, they suddenly became aware of a white male coming out of the pub a little way up the street.

Both melted into the shadows and waited. They didn't want to be seen by anybody in the area.

As they watched, they were both pleasantly surprised to see this person stop at number 42 and start fumbling with the front door key, trying to get it into the lock.

They both nodded to each other and silently approached the man just as he managed to open the door.

Ritchie moved with the speed of a big cat and pushed him face first into the passageway.

By the time Finlay Bryant staggered to his feet, the hall light was on and two menacing looking men had shut the door and were looming over him.

"Who the fuck are..."

Finlay's words were cut short by a heavy backhanded slap from the bald-headed man with the red scar down his face.

Finlay stagged back and fell onto the bottom step of the staircase. Fear was in his eyes as he tasted the coppery tang of blood in his mouth.

The other man, who was older but no less intimating, stepped forward.

"What's your name, son?"

Finlay was shaking badly and his voice quivered as he answered.

"Finlay Bryant."

"Right, Fin. May I call you Fin?" asked the older man.

Finlay nodded dumbly.

"Right, simple answer to a simple question. Where is Tommy Scott?"

"Who?" answered Finlay.

The man's face broke into a smile that reminded him of a great white shark closing for the kill.

"Fin, I thought this was going to be simple. So, I will ask you again. Where is Tommy?"

Fin once more played dumb.

Ronnie nodded to Ritchie.

The bald-headed man moved quickly yet again and smashed a fist into Finlay's face, breaking his nose.

Finlay cried out as blood spurted from the wound.

"Last chance, boy," said Ronnie.

Fin didn't reply.

Ronnie nodded again to Ritchie.

Ritchie grabbed Finlay's right hand and snapped his little finger.

Finlay screamed out in pain

"I will ask you again, Fin; otherwise, another finger goes. I know you have met up and I know he is staying here. So, where is he now?" asked Ronnie.

Through tears of pain, Finlay still denied knowing Tommy.

Ritchie took out the ring finger.

Finlay was nearly passing out with the pain.

Ronnie looked down at the pathetic figure curled up on the ground.

"I can make all this pain go away if you just tell me the truth."

Finlay sobbed pitifully, but said nothing.

Ritchie now grabbed him by the left ear and stretched it out, reaching into his pocket for his favourite weapon. The Stanley knife.

"You are about to lose an ear, my son," snarled Ronnie.

The blade began to slowly cut.

"Alright! Alright!" screamed Finlay, "He was here, but we had an argument and he went off. I don't know where he went."

Ronnie contemplated this.

Suddenly, there was a knock on the door.

Ritchie headed to it.

Finlay cried out in desperation as he knew Tommy would come looking for him because he had been away from the pub too long.

As Ritchie opened the door, Finlay shouted out.

"Run, Tomo! Run for your life!"

The door opened to reveal Marcus Campbell not Tommy.

Finlay looked up at the huge black guy framing the doorway.

"Who the fuck is this?" the man asked.

"This, my friend, is the man who is about to tell me where Tommy is or he will suffer a slow and painful end."

Marcus smiled and gave Ronnie the car keys.

Ritchie moved forward once again, brandishing the Stanley knife whose blade was slick with blood.

Ronnie regarded Finlay.

"Finish him, but make it clean. No knives."

Ritchie seemed disappointed.

He hurled Finlay to his feet.

"Please, please," he begged in fear.

* * *

Tommy looked at his watch. Where the fuck had Finlay got to? He had been gone ages.

Probably lit up one of his joints and fell asleep, the twat, he concluded.

Tommy decided to phone him.

That is when he noticed that his phone was now on five percent.

He decided to go find Finlay and also hopefully find a phone charger in his house.

Tommy headed to the side door, slipped the bolt and went out into the cold night air.

He looked towards Finlay's house and saw a man stood in the doorway.

Tommy had a sinking feeling in his stomach.

He gingerly stepped forward and that was when the man turned and saw him.

Tommy instantly recognised that it was Marcus Campbell.

* * *

"Boss, there he is!" shouted Marcus pointing at Tommy who had already broken into a run.

The big black man moved quickly to give chase.

Ronnie Moon glanced at Ritchie.

"You wait here. I'm going to get the car and follow them."

Ritchie nodded, went back inside and shut the door.

Finlay looked up pleadingly at the bald man, but only saw dead, emotionless eyes staring back at him.

Ritchie Cummings grabbed a handful of Finlay's greasy hair.

"Please, man. Please don't," pleaded Finlay.

His pleas fell on deaf ears as Ritchie span him around like a rag doll, gripped his chin and viciously wrenched it around, snapping Finlay's neck like a twig.

His limp body fell to the carpet.

Ritchie stood back out of the way and watched fascinatedly as the light faded out of the dying man's eyes. When he was sure he was dead, he searched the dead man's pockets and took his mobile phone.

He now headed to the kitchen to look for some black dustbin liners and something to clean up the mess.

But first, he would put the kettle on. He was dying for a cuppa.

All this exercise had given him a raging thirst.

Chapter 13

Tommy broke into a sprint and headed down the street past the pub. He wasn't exactly sure where he was heading, but right now, keeping a distance between himself and Marcus 'Mad Dog' Campbell was his priority.

Marcus was a big unit, but Tommy felt the big man might just run out of steam if he kept the pace up.

He momentarily thought of Finlay. He prayed that his friend was okay, but way down in the pit of his stomach, he knew that probably wasn't the case.

Tommy glanced back and saw Marcus still in pursuit. In his panic, all thought of his scooter went out of his head.

He turned right across from the pub and ran on. He noticed to his left a series of allotments. Beyond them was the local railway track. If he could get there, he felt sure he could lose his tail.

He turned left and ran hard towards the allotment gates.

His lungs were burning with the exhaustion.

At school, he used to love cross country running, but too many ensuing years of abuse to his body had now taken its toll. He just prayed he had enough in his tank to outrun the monster pursuing him.

***

Ronnie gunned the Mercedes down the street, but was careful not to speed and bring attention to himself.

Way up ahead, he could see Marcus. He kept his speed steady and followed.

They would soon have Tommy.

* * *

Tommy ran towards the gates and guessed they would be locked. He was going to have to climb over them and hope that Marcus wouldn't be able to follow likewise.

He dared not look back over his shoulder. He had to just go for it.

At full sprint, he reached the gates, jumped up and started climbing.

He would have easily got over them before Marcus caught up, but unfortunately for him, his jacket snagged on a nail halfway up and it cost him precious seconds trying to unhook it.

By the time he had freed himself, Marcus was at the gate.

The big man was sweating and breathing heavily.

It didn't stop him making a grab for Tommy's leg.

Tommy kicked back, avoiding being grabbed.

"Fuck you, you big fuck. You ain't getting your fat ass over this gate," shouted Tommy.

The adrenaline rushing through his veins had given him a 'splash of the bold', as the wine advert said.

Marcus looked up at Tommy with a death stare.

"Pretty brave up there, aren't you? But don't be too fucking cocky, boy."

With that, the big man stepped back and ran, then surprisingly sprung up onto the gate like a panther.

It shook under his weight and Tommy lost his grip momentarily and slipped down a little.

He regained his hold, but this also allowed Marcus to reach into his coat pocket and take out a black oblong object. Tommy didn't know what it was until Marcus pressed a button and a crackle of blue electric radiated from the end.

A stun gun.

Marcus 'Mad Dog' Campbell's weapon of choice.

As Marcus lunged up with the gun, Tommy had an extra surge of strength and found himself at the top of the gate.

Without hesitating, he went over and dropped off the other side and disappeared like a hare across the allotments.

Marcus watched from the top of the gate as Tommy disappeared. He knew he wouldn't catch him now.

"You can't run forever. I will find you."

He dropped back to the ground cursing and pocketed the stun gun. How he would have liked to press it onto that bastard Tommy's neck or balls and hear him scream.

Never mind. He would get his chance.

Just then, the Mercedes pulled up and Ronnie lowered the driver's window.

"Any luck, Marcus?"

"No, boss. He got too much of a head start on me. I think he is heading for the railway lines though."

Ronnie cursed under his breath.

"Okay. We can't get down to the tracks in a car. Hop in and we'll go back to the house for Ritchie and make another plan from there."

***

Tommy ran through the allotments and climbed another fence that brought him out onto the railway lines. The track was a local branch line, not a main one, and at this time of the morning nothing would be running.

He was safe to walk along it. Plus, he wasn't going to be surprised by a car suddenly coming at him. That said, he still warily looked around him expecting Marcus, Ritchie or Ronnie to explode from the undergrowth.

That had been a close call and he had been lucky to get a head start on Marcus. That motherfucker was scary.

Concerned about Fin, he decided to ring his friend's number before his phone completely died. It just went to answerphone. Not a good sign.

He left a message.

Fin. If you can, ring or text me that you are okay, will you? Tomo.

He wanted to ring Sharon to see if she was also alright. For Ronnie to come to Fin's house, she must have told him his whereabouts. He hoped and prayed there had been no violence as she was Ronnie's sister.

He hesitated over ringing in case Ronnie and his cronies had gone back to his house and were waiting for his call. Although it was dangerous, he decided to chance what would probably be his final text for now.

Hi Sharon, I'm okay. Ronnie and his boys came visiting, but I got away. I will have to lie low for now until I can get to meet this guy who took the money. I pray you are not hurt. Just message me an x to tell me you are fine. Love you. P.S. My phone is about to die. I will need to find a charger.

A moment later, Tommy's phone pinged back with a text.

X.

She was safe. He breathed a sigh of relief.

* * *

The three men took the Mercedes around the streets in the surrounding area, but with no luck.

"Bollocks," growled Ronnie.

His eyes scoured the streets like a hungry lion who had just lost its prey.

In the back seat, a mobile pinged a voicemail.

Ritchie took out the phone and read it. He smiled to himself.

"All might not be lost, boss," he said.

"Why's that, Ritchie?"

"Well, I picked up the dead man's phone back at the house. Just on impulse. It wasn't locked. Tommy, with his sense of conscience, has just left a voicemail."

Ritchie listened to the message and grinned.

"He is asking his mate to confirm he is okay."

Ronnie turned around to face the man in the backseat.

"So, what you are saying is he doesn't suspect he's dead, right?"

Ritchie nodded.

"Yeah, that's right. So, if I text him back pretending to be this Fin geezer and tell him I'm alright and to come back and meet him at the house, then there is a good chance he will come."

"He might smell a rat," said Marcus.

"It's got to be worth a try, hasn't it?" answered Ritchie.

Ronnie nodded in agreement.

"Do it and let's see if the bastard goes for it."

Ritchie began texting.

* * *

Adam Lucas couldn't sleep. After tossing and turning for what seemed like hours, he slipped out of bed leaving Jackie sleeping and went downstairs to the living room.

He poured himself a scotch and stood looking out of the window in the kitchen onto the back garden. His thoughts kept returning to the cash in the garage.

If he was going to keep it, he had to find a way to launder it. It would mean involving his uncle Frank. The less people who knew about the money, the better, but he didn't have a clue what to do otherwise.

In this day and age now, cash was a dirty word and very hard to get rid of without drawing suspicion.

Holidays could be paid for in cash, filling up the car, meals out, clothes, household goods, but you had no chance with big stuff.

Even gambling these days didn't deal in ready money as they did years ago.

He took a sip of his drink.

Maybe he should just return it and forget all about it?

Money – a curse if you have it; a curse if you don't.

For now, he would just have to keep hold of it and see what happened.

He would have to eventually tell Jackie.

Adam took another gulp of scotch.

That was not a conversation he was looking forward to.

He finished his drink and slowly headed back upstairs, hoping sleep would come to give his mind a rest.

* * *

Tommy regarded the text message. At first, his hopes were raised, but when he read it again, something didn't seem right.

Hi Tommy, I'm alright. A few bumps and bruises, but nothing more. I'm at the house. I don't think they'll come back here tonight. Get back over here when you can. I'll keep an eye out for you.

Tommy looked at the wording. Something troubled him.

Fin usually referred to him as Tomo, never Tommy.

But maybe he was frightened and had just become more formal.

Even so....

Tommy was torn between what to do, but his need to know if his friend was truly okay overrode his suspicion. He would head back to Herald Way and chance it.

Tommy texted back.

On my way. I'll be about twenty minutes or so.

Chapter 14

Inside number 42 Herald Way, Ritchie and Marcus moved the body of Finlay Bryant into the boot of the Mercedes, which was parked around the back of the house. It was wrapped heavily in black dustbin liners and taped up. They would dispose of it later.

Next, they went into the front room, pulled the curtains, put on the lamp and switched on the television. Anybody arriving at the house would presume from the outside that the owner was having a night in watching the TV.

That was the impression they wanted to give.

Ronnie sat in the armchair by the fireplace and Ritchie and Marcus sat on the settee.

The three men were silent, all half-heartedly watching a rerun on Challenge of *Bullseye*.

"What a load of shit prizes on here," mused Marcus.

Ronnie smiled.

"Not back then it wasn't. Times change."

It had been ten minutes since the return text from Tommy.

He would be here soon.

This time, Ronnie was not letting him get away until he found out what had happened to his money.

* * *

Lisa Miller staggered out of the side door of the *Turk's Head*. She supported herself against the doorframe and hiccupped.

The cold air hitting her suddenly made her feel nauseous.

She had really given the G&T a hammering tonight.

Lisa now searched in her bag for her cigarettes and realised that she had smoked the last one a little while back.

Shit, she would kill for a fag.

She wondered where Fin had got to as she had paid him for some weed.

She looked up the street and saw the light on in Fin's house.

Great, he was still up.

Lisa lived at 48 Herald Way. She had been a neighbour of Fin's for a few years now. She had also at one time been his on/off lover, but not anymore.

Lisa had a new man in her life these days. John Baron. He was away at present working on the oil rigs, but was due back Tuesday. Lisa couldn't wait for him to return. She got lonely on her own. Hence, this big Sunday night out.

It was handy having the pub on the doorstep. No expensive cab fares home and no long walks the wrong side of midnight.

She decided to give Finlay's door a knock and see if she could bum a fag and get her shit. Knowing the dirty little bastard, he would want something extra in return.

Well, she might succumb to giving him a hand job, but that was where she would draw the line. She was John's girl now and spoken for.

She took a deep breath and tried to focus her eyes on number 42 and begin to weave a path towards it.

Definitely too much gin.

* * *

Tommy watched the house from the other side of the road. The curtains were drawn and the lights were on in the front downstairs room.

He had scoured the nearby streets to see if he could find Ronnie's Mercedes parked up, but found nothing. That didn't mean they weren't in the house waiting for him.

Part of him wanted to text Finlay and tell him he was outside, but his phone was completely dead. Another part of him was worried that it wasn't Fin answering his phone anyway.

Tommy was torn between knocking on the door or just disappearing into the night.

He then saw a woman staggering along the pavement and recognised her as Lisa Miller, Fin's neighbour that they had bumped into earlier in the pub.

Tommy quickly stepped out of the shadows and called her name as carefully as he could without shouting.

Lisa looked across the road towards him.

"Who is it?" she asked.

Her voice was slurred.

"It's Tommy, Fin's mate. We met earlier in the pub. Remember?"

Lisa thought for a moment.

"Oh yeah. I remember."

"Lisa, can you come over here a minute?"

She eyed him suspiciously.

"Why? What are you up to?"

"I need your help. Just come over here, will you?"

Tommy nervously glanced at number 42 and thought he saw the curtains twitch.

Lisa staggered over the road to Tommy. He grabbed her arm and led her around the corner out of sight.

She pulled away from his grip.

"Hey, what is this all about? I don't want any funny business here."

Tommy explained without too much detail that some men were after him and they had come to Fin's looking for him. He suspected that Fin could be hurt and the men could still be in the house. He needed to know if his friend was okay or that the men were inside.

Lisa swayed back and forth as she listened. She sort of got the picture.

"Well, I was just about to go ask him for some weed he owes me, so I suppose I could do that. What do you think?"

"Okay. That's a good idea. Go do it. If he is in, cool. If somebody else answers, make your excuses and leave," replied Tommy.

Lisa made to walk off and then looked back.

"Just how dangerous are these men if they are in there?"

"They're not dangerous to you if you just follow what I've told you."

Lisa looked at Tommy as if trying to see if she could read his mind.

She then nodded and headed back across the road.

* * *

Marcus pulled back the curtain carefully and glanced out.

"No sign of him yet. Wait up. There's some tart approaching the house. Looks like she's pissed out of her brain."

"Who is she?" asked Ritchie.

Marcus carried on watching her.

"How the fuck do I know, bro? I'm not a mind reader."

Ritchie now joined him at the window.

"Bit of alright by the look of her."

Marcus grinned.

"Christ, Ritchie you would fuck anything that has a pulse."

Ritchie laughed.

"Bollocks. You aren't exactly a monk yourself."

There was a knock on the front door.

Nobody moved.

The knocking came again.

Ronnie looked up from his seat.

"Get rid of her quickly or she is going to fuck everything up."

Marcus nodded and headed for the door.

***

Lisa was surprised to see the door opened by a large, intimidating but good-looking black man.

"Yes?" he asked.

After a brief pause, Lisa found her voice.

"Is Fin about? I'm a neighbour, Lisa."

"He had to nip out. I don't know when he'll be back,' replied Marcus.

Lisa steadied herself on the doorframe.

"Who are you then, handsome? I haven't seen you around here before."

"Just a mate visiting."

Lisa regarded the man.

There was no more information forthcoming. She didn't like the vibe coming off of this guy.

"Right. Well, I'll call tomorrow."

"Yeah. Good idea, Lisa. Goodnight now."

Lisa nodded and stole a quick glance into the hallway. She glimpsed another person coming down the stairs. Before she could look again, the man shut the door.

She looked across the road to the shadows and shook her head, hoping that Tommy would see. She couldn't risk going any closer as she was sure she was being watched from the house. Lisa now turned and headed for her home.

Tommy had seen Marcus come to the door. So, they were back in the house waiting for him to slip up and return. Well, fuck them. He wasn't going to fall into their trap. He was sorry that Fin had been involved. He had a bad feeling about him.

The question was where was he going to go now?

* * *

Marcus came back into the living room.

"She gone?" asked Ronnie.

"Yeah, but she's an inquisitive cow," replied Marcus.

"I reckon she'll phone the coppers."

Ronnie looked concerned.

He got up from his chair and paced the living room.

"I don't think the bastard is going to come back. We'll catch up with him again. For now, we need to clean this place up and get rid of the body. Marcus, go and see if that girl is still on the street. If she contacts the police, she'll give a pretty good description of you. Nothing must be traced back to me. To all intents and purposes, I am at home in the Cotswolds with Josie and nowhere near Bristol. Understand?"

Marcus nodded.

* * *

From the shadows, Tommy watched Lisa searching in her bag for presumably her house keys. It was one hell of a drunken performance. Once she was inside, he would leave.

He suddenly remembered his scooter, which was parked down the side road by the *Turk's Head*.

If Ronnie and his boys were staying put, maybe he might get back home to see Sharon. Maybe?

Suddenly, the front door of 42 opened and Marcus Campbell walked out.

Lisa was too preoccupied to see him.

Tommy had a bad feeling about this, but if he shouted a warning to her, he would give himself away.

Not for the first time tonight, he agonised on his decision.

Lisa then found the keys and inserted them in the lock, but Marcus was nearly on her.

Tommy looked around him and saw a recycling box outside a house nearby. It was full of empty wine and spirit bottles. The residents of the house must have recently had a party.

Tommy ran and grabbed one of the heavy spirit bottles.

***

Marcus came up behind Lisa and effortlessly wrapped his left arm around her neck and squeezed tightly. The pure strength and know-how of the man put her out like a light. Holding the girl's limp body in one arm, he reached for the key that was still in the lock with his other hand and turned it, but the lock seemed to be sticking.

He tried again, but at that moment, he felt something solid explode on the back of his head making him see stars. Marcus let go of the girl and she slumped to the pavement.

He turned around in pain just as Tommy swung the bottle again, catching him on the temple. Things now began to turn black as Marcus felt his legs giving way. A third blow square between the eyes sent him to the ground semi-unconscious.

Tommy was shaking like a leaf. Adrenaline was coursing through his veins at a great rate of knots. He dropped the bottle down and went to Lisa. She was coming around.

"Quick. Get to your feet. Hurry," pleaded Tommy.

He glanced at number 42, expecting any moment for Ronnie to appear along with that lunatic Cummings.

Tommy lifted Lisa up to her feet. She was confused but coherent.

"Have you somewhere you can stay tonight?" he asked.

He could now see fear in her eyes as she was rapidly sobering up.

"Ah yes, my friend Carrie. She lives a short way from here."

"Right. Come with me now before this joker wakes up."

"Okay, Tommy."

Tommy smiled weakly at her.

They ran down the road to the scooter.

"Right. Hold me tight and give me directions to this Carrie's."

They headed off into the night.

Once he had dropped Lisa off, he decided his best course of action was to get a room at a Travelodge or its like. Lie low and then get to the Memorial Park tomorrow. It was too risky to head home.

He was sure this would be Ronnie's next port of call.

He was tired and hungry and had enough excitement for one day.

He started up the scooter and disappeared into the night.

* * *

With the house cleaned up and the body safely in the boot of the car, Ritchie drove the Mercedes around to the front of the house just in time to see Marcus stagger up to it. The black man slipped into the back seat looking a little worse for wear.

"What the fuck happened to you?" asked Ritchie, "Don't tell me the tart beat you up?"

Marcus glared at the other man.

"Don't be a prick, Ritchie. Fucking Tommy blindsided me and hit me with an empty bottle of some sorts. Knocked me cold. My head hurts like a bitch."

Ritchie couldn't help giggling.

Ronnie spoke.

"Well, well, well. Our Tommy has some balls after all. This makes things interesting."

Ritchie regarded him.

"Where to now, boss?"

Ronnie sighed.

"We'll call it a night and look tomorrow. Drop me back at my sister's, will you? And pick me up 9.00am sharp in the morning. I think our next move is to visit this *Luggage Safe* and see if the money was picked up in the first place and if it has, was it Tommy who picked it up?"

Ritchie nodded.

"Oh yeah. On the way home, let's find somewhere suitable to dump the body."

As they pulled away from the kerb, they could hear a police car siren getting closer.

Ronnie regarded Ritchie.

"Time to put your foot down and make some distance between us and them. Looks like a neighbour has called the Old Bill."

Chapter 15

Next morning at 10.00am, Ronnie, Marcus and Ritchie walked into *Luggage Safe*. Emily was on the front desk and just finishing off with a customer.

She saw the three men come in and, for some reason, alarm bells sounded. There was something about them that she didn't like. To her, they looked like heavy-duty villains.

Although she was only going on her experience of seeing them on television shows. Being professional, she didn't want to make abrupt assumptions.

She took a deep breath and acknowledged them.

"Good morning. How can I help you?" she asked.

Ronnie was all smiles.

"Good morning, love. I'm thinking of depositing a suitcase in here and I wondered if I might be able to speak to the manager as the case is rather important."

Emily smiled back sweetly.

"I'm afraid he's busy at present, but I can answer any of your queries."

The smile was still pasted on Ronnie's feature.

"I'm sure you can."

Ronnie paused to look at her name badge pinned to the lapel of her smart blazer.

"I'm sure you can, Emily. But no disrespect, I need to see the manager."

"Well, in that case, sir, you will need to make an appointment."

Ronnie's smile faded.

"Now that is a problem because I am only in Bristol today on business. So, I would be extremely grateful if you could ask him if he would have time to see me now."

Emily suddenly didn't like the tone of the man's voice. The other two drew closer like a pair of stalking lions.

Emily swallowed hard, trying to keep her composure.

"Well, I will go and ask him, but I can't promise anything."

"I would be grateful," replied Ronnie.

Emily disappeared into the back room.

The men looked around the shop and found it at present empty of any other customers. Marcus turned the open sign around to closed and pulled down the blind. They made their way around the counter and headed back behind the scenes.

As they arrived in the area where the storage lockers were located, a young man who was working close by looked up and was startled to see them standing there.

"Excuse me. This is a private area here. Staff only."

Ronnie reached in his pocket and flashed a card.

"Inland Revenue, sir. Come to see your boss. Carry on as you are."

The man looked suspicious.

"Can I have a closer look at those credentials, please?

Ronnie nodded and handed the card to Marcus who walked over to the man and held it out to him.

The man leaned in closely to read it. That was when Marcus planted a left hook on his jaw that knocked him out immediately.

Marcus dragged him out of sight.

The three men now walked down the corridor until they arrived at a door with the sign 'Manager' written on it .

Emily was just coming out the door and was shocked to see them standing there.

"You shouldn't be back here. Anyway, Leon, the manager, is busy."

Ritchie swiftly picked her up like a rag doll and carried her off.

"I will keep an eye on her, boss."

He disappeared into another office, which was empty.

***

Leon was just having a first bite of a jam doughnut when the door opened and two men walked in.

Through a mouthful of jam and sugar, he spluttered.

"Excuse me .You can't just walk in here and…"

Ronnie cut him off.

"Shut the fuck up, fat boy, or I'll shove that doughnut straight up your ass. You will be shitting sugar and jam for a week."

Leon dropped the doughnut on his desk and sat back in his chair.

He had a feeling where this conversation was heading, especially as the other man turned the key in his office door locking it firmly shut.

Leon made a grab for the telephone on his desk, but the black man moved with the speed of a panther.

Leon felt an electric shock run through his body as the man drove some sort of object into his bare arm.

The phone dropped instantly, and Leon writhed in pain.

The older man spoke again.

"Right, behave yourself and answer our questions and you just might not feel the pain of my friend's stun gun on your flesh again. Fuck me about and the next place you will feel it is on your scrotum. Understand?"

Leon nodded dumbly.

"I had a bag deposited here in locker 79 a few days ago. Is that bag still here?"

Leon knew right away what bag it was, but he stalled for time.

"I need to check the computer. May I?"

Ronnie nodded.

Leon made a pretence of tapping in on the keys.

After a moment, he answered.

"No, it's not here now. It was picked up."

Ronnie got out his phone and scrolled to a photo of Tommy Scott.

"Was this the man who picked it up?"

Leon recognised the agitated man who had threatened him yesterday.

Fuck it, he had no love lost for this jerk.

"Yes, that was him. I served him myself," he answered.

"Are you sure?" asked Ronnie.

"Yes, I am positive."

Ronnie eyes burnt into Leon's as if searching his very soul.

Leon held his nerve.

He stared back at Ronnie.

"Why? Is there some sort of problem?"

Ronnie broke his gaze.

"Not if what you say is true. Then there is no problem. But if I find out you're lying, I will come back here and find you and hold you personally responsible. Do I make myself clear, fat boy?"

Leon felt he was dying inside.

"Yes, perfectly."

Marcus unlocked the door .

Ronnie walked towards it, then stopped and looked back.

"Do not think of calling the police. If you do, somebody will find you and break every bone in your body."

Leon nodded and watched the men begin to leave.

His mind worked fast.

"What if this guy has taken your bag, but denies he picked it up?"

Ronnie looked back at Leon.

"When we catch up with him, believe me, we will get the truth out of him and if it is you who is lying, we will be back."

The men left his office.

When they had gone, Leon sank his head in his hands.

He knew that there would be comeback. You just don't steal that amount of money without consequence.

These men looked seriously dangerous.

Adam and he were way out of their depth.

He needed to call Adam now and tell him to bring the money back.

He could always manufacture some story of mistake and confusion and just give the money back when these men came calling again, which he knew they would eventually.

He reached for his mobile and called Adam's number.

***

Adam heard his phone ring and checked the caller ID. It was Leon. He would have to wait as it was 10.55am and he was just at the gates of Hawthorne Memorial Park.

The small park was a memorial to local men who had fought as soldiers in World War Two. There was a memorial cross in the centre of the gardens where wreaths were regularly placed.

Various flower beds and benches were dotted around the rest of the area.

The sheltered seating was at the back of the park and was regularly used by the homeless or amorous courting couples.

He headed towards it and saw that Rat was already there. Adam drew closer and saw Rat was sipping on a *McDonald's* coffee.

"Morning, Rat. How's it going?"

Rat smiled at Adam.

"All good, my friend. Grab a seat."

Adam sat down next to him.

"Right. What can I help you with today? And I take it the twenty is still on offer?"

Adam nodded, reached in his pocket and produced the £20 note and handed it over.

Rat took it and quickly put it away inside the many folds of his garments.

The morning air was crisp and cold, and Adam wished he had stopped to pick up a coffee himself.

Before Adam spoke, Rat cut in.

"Adam, I met a couple of men last night that were mighty keen to find you."

Adam's heart quickened. He tried to remain cool.

"Oh yeah. Who were they?"

"An old mate of mine, a Finlay Bryant, and a friend of his called Tomo or Tommy Scott."

Adam shrugged his shoulder.

"Can't say I've heard of them."

"That's funny because they said they were old mates of yours."

Adam shook his head.

"No. Their names don't ring a bell."

Rat smiled.

"What's the game, Adam? I want in. I smell money here."

"I don't know what you mean, Rat."

"Come on, man. Don't kid a kidder. What's going down?"

"Nothing. Now, are we going to talk or not? I want my money's worth."

Rat sipped his coffee.

"Well, we might not have time as this Tommy Scott character will be here any second to speak to you."

Adam jumped up and looked around.

"You sold me out! Why was I paying you!" Adam shouted.

Rat regarded him.

' "Nothing personal, man. But I have got to survive however I can. Your book could be just pie in the sky that never exactly transpires. This Tommy paid me good money to find you. Now, if you want to pay me more, maybe you can get away before he shows."

Adam laughed.

"How about I just walk now and fuck you, you Judas."

Adam made to walk off, but from the bushes stepped two men.

"These are my friends, Axel and Joel."

The men walked forward. Both brandished knives.

* * *

Tommy was running late. He had slept in as he had been so exhausted. He had plugged his phone in once he was in his room at the Travelodge, but stupidly forget to set the alarm.

He was now going as fast as the scooter would let him up from the city centre to Gloucester Road.

The traffic was busy as he weaved in and out of it.

Shit, he hoped that he wouldn't miss them.

He now approached the bottom of Gloucester Road and began his uphill ride.

Tommy gunned the scooter up the outside of a traffic jam, passing vehicle after vehicle.

He glanced at his watch. 11.05am. He just might be okay. The park wasn't far away now.

Suddenly, in front of him, a parked car swung open its door and Tommy ploughed straight into it.

He went flying off the scooter to land in a heap on the tarmac.

Pain shot up his left arm and shoulder where he had landed on it heavily.

Incensed, he scrambled to his feet and turned to face the driver of the car.

"You stupid fucker. You could have killed me, you careless..."

His words froze in his throat as he confronted the menacing form of Ritchie Cummings.

"Shut the fuck up and get in the car, Tommy."

Tommy turned to run, but ran straight into Marcus, who kneed him immediately in the balls, incapacitating him.

Marcus dragged the limp figure of Tommy Scott to the open back door, pushed him into the back seat and immediately got in behind him.

Tommy looked up to see Ronnie Moon looking at him from the front passenger seat.

"Well, well, well. At last, we've found you and what a stroke of luck. We only pulled in here to get some of my cigars in the newsagents and, out of the blue, God delivers you on a plate for me. I stayed at yours last night. Sharon sends her love, by the way. She is fine, but a little worried I might hurt you."

Ronnie laughed chillingly and then added, "Now, where's my money?"

Before Tommy could answer, Marcus pushed the stun gun into his ribs and gave him a shot of electric. Tommy howled in pain and cowered away to the far seat.

Marcus smiled.

"That was for hitting me one last night, you little shit, and there is more to come unless you answer the boss's questions."

Tommy held up his hands.

"Look, I'm on my way now to get it. Honestly."

Ronnie stared at him.

"Explain."

"I will, Ronnie, but can we drive; otherwise, I am going to miss the meet. It's just up the road at Hawthorne Memorial Park."

Ronnie nodded to Ritchie.

The Mercedes pulled away from the kerb.

He then addressed Tommy.

"Right, get talking and this better be good. You are already down for a beating. What you tell me may determine whether you live or not."

* * *

Adam looked at the two men coming at him. They both looked haggard and desperate. Drug addicts, he deduced. Men willing to go to any extremes for a fix.

He looked towards Rat.

"What is this? I thought we had an understanding. A deal."

Rat smiled.

"That is where you are naïve, boy. The only law on the streets of the homeless is survival."

The men edged closer.

"What is it you want? More money? Well, I can get you that. No problem. I have plenty to spare."

"Is that so? Well, for you to come to no harm and for me to tell Tommy and Fin you didn't turn up for our meeting, I want a grand."

"Alright. You can have your grand. No. Fuck it. Let's make it two, shall we?"

Rat's eyes shone with glee.

He had hit the fucking jackpot.

Adam continued.

"I haven't got it on me, but I can take you to it."

Rat contemplated this for a moment.

"Okay. Let's make a move sharpish before…"

Rat was stopped in mid-sentence.

Ritchie had appeared from behind the shelter and pulled a plastic bag tightly over his head. Rat thrashed about, trying to first claw at the bag and then his attacker.

His struggles were futile.

Tommy Scott walked forward.

They had all arrived unnoticed and heard the dialogue between Rat and Adam.

It had tied in with what Tommy had told them in the car.

"You greedy fucking Judas. This is what happens for selling me down the river," said Tommy.

From behind the plastic, Rat's eyes stared pleadingly.

The bag remained firm.

Soon, his oxygen supply was cut off and he collapsed unconscious to the floor.

The two men, Axel and Joel, turned to run, but the mountainous figure of Marcus stood before them blocking their escape.

Before they could react, Marcus slammed the edge of his hand across Axel's neck, nearly scything the man's head off his shoulders. He dropped instantly unconscious to the ground like a dead thing.

Joel panicked and slashed at Marcus with his knife.

The big man blocked the scrawny knife arm with his own forearm and brought his other stiffened forearm up under Joel's elbow snapping it like a carrot. He next kicked down through the man's knee, snapping the ligaments like elastic bands. As Joel fell to the ground screaming, Marcus football kicked his head, which silenced him.

The execution of the beating was precise and savage.

Adam went to run, but he didn't see Ronnie behind.

The older man grabbed Adam by the coat lapel in a tight grip and drove an uppercut punch into his solar plexus, which dropped him to his knees. His diaphragm spasmed as he was sick on the grass.

He waited helplessly for the follow-up blow, but it never came.

Ritchie and Marcus dragged him to his feet and shoved him down on a bench.

Ronnie grabbed him by the hair and yanked his head back so he could look into Adam's eyes.

"Right, you thieving little shit. My name is Ronnie Moon. Your worst nightmare. Now, where is my fucking money?" he snarled.

Chapter 16

Jackie Lucas rummaged around in the garage. She was sure there was half a tin of grey paint out here somewhere.

She had been meaning to paint a wicker chair, which she bought in a charity shop some time ago. It would look perfect in the nursery and ideal for sitting on and feeding the baby at night.

Jackie had been putting off the task for some while now. She always convinced herself that she was busy with something else. Today, she was determined to do it if she could find the damn paint. No more excuses.

Jackie was finding the going getting tougher every week.

As she got bigger, she struggled to do chores that normally she would whiz through.

She always felt tired these days. She would be glad when the baby was born and she could get back to the gym and out running again.

Puffing her way up and down the stairs and needing Adam to get her in and out the bath were not dignified things she relished. Painting her toenails were out of the question and trying to put on a pair of socks was a major task.

* * *

She had checked on the shelves and the work bench and even in the old metal upright filing cabinet that used to be in the spare bedroom when they used it for an office. Now she moved away some boxes and sacking by the work bench.

That is when she discovered the bag.

Strange. It looked new. She couldn't remember Adam buying it.

She picked it up. It was weighty. She needed both hands to heft it up onto the work bench.

What could be in it?

Jackie went to open it, but then thought that there might be a secret gift in it for her from Adam and he was hiding it.

She hesitated, but then noticed the label on the bag.

Luggage Safe.

Wasn't that where Adam's best mate, Leon, worked?

Yes, it was. Adam was always down there at least once a month for a coffee and a chat with Leon.

Maybe he was storing something for his friend?

She looked at the bag again. Curiosity got the better of her. She couldn't help it.

As a child around Christmas time, she always hunted high and low for her Christmas presents and was usually scolded by her parents about it.

Even now around her birthday, she would search in Adam's wardrobe for a hidden present.

She wasn't great at waiting. Hence, the need for this baby to be born.

Drawing back the zip, Jackie pulled open the bag and gasped in shock and surprise at the money inside. She stared at it for what seemed like an hour and then gingerly pulled out a stack and ran her fingers through it.

My God, where had it come from? And what's more, what was Adam doing with it?

Her mind swirled with all sorts of possibilities.

She pulled her phone out of her dress pocket and rang Adam's number.

Jackie sat down on an upturned crate as she did so. She felt a little faint.

It went to answerphone.

She cursed.

She couldn't wait for Adam to come home. He had mentioned that he might stay out the night on the streets.

Jackie considered her options and then thought of Leon. She rang his number and he answered almost immediately.

"Hi, Jackie. Nice to hear from you. Is everything okay?"

'Leon, I know this might sound strange, but I've found a bag of money in our garage, which has come from *Luggage Safe*. I don't know how it got here and I'm scared. What the hell is going on? Do you know?"

Leon breathed a sigh of resignation.

"Jackie, is Adam there?"

"No, I'm on my own."

"Right. Can you bring it to me and I will explain everything?"

"Adam has the car," Jackie replied.

"Get a taxi straight here. I'll stand the fare here and back. And whatever you do, don't mention the money to anybody else."

Jackie disconnected the call.

She now phoned for a taxi.

Next, she grabbed the bag, went back into the house, slipped on her coat and picked up her keys.

She waited by the open front door until she saw the taxi pull up outside.

Jackie wondered what the hell was going on here. She needed some answers fast.

* * *

Adam sat between Ritchie and Marcus in the back seat of the Mercedes. Tommy was now in the front passenger seat and Ronnie was driving.

The car's sat nav was on and taking them to the address that Adam had given them.

The three men were silent in the back.

Adam knew the game was up and the fleeting fortune was not coming his way. That was one thing. But he was more worried about what would happen to him once these men had collected the money.

He thought of Jackie and the baby.

He hoped to God that she wasn't in and maybe had visited a friend.

What the hell was she going to make of all this? Plus, he didn't want her or his unborn child hurt in any way.

He wondered if he would be around to see the baby born.

Tears had begun to sting his eyes.

Why had he done it?

He had wanted a better life for Jackie, him and the baby.

A life where they didn't have to scrimp and safe. One where they didn't have to count every penny. Where he didn't lie in bed at night worrying constantly about their finances.

Alright, it had been utter madness, but for a moment, he had lived a dream. Now, it had turned into a nightmare.

He glanced left and right at the two men sat next to him. Both stared ahead. They were stone-cold killers; he had witnessed that in the Memorial Park first hand.

He prayed that his life might be spared.

The older man sat in the driver's seat. This Ronnie Moon didn't look the forgiving sort.

***

Ronnie glanced over at Tommy. He spoke quietly.

"This isn't over for you, my son. When I get this money back, you will still have to answer for your fuckup."

Tommy stared straight ahead out of the window.

He couldn't look Ronnie in the face.

There was nothing to say.

He had blown it big time.

Tommy knew payment was going to be painful.

Closing his eyes, he lent back against the headrest.

Inside, all he could think about was Sharon and the hurt he had caused her over the years.

Maybe he didn't deserve to live.

***

The taxi dropped Jackie outside Bristol Temple Meads and she made her way across the road to *News Plus*.

Struggling to carry the bag, she made her way through the shop to *Luggage Safe*.

Leon Biggs was waiting for her on the counter.

When he saw her struggling with the bag, he immediately came around and took it off of her and then ushered her around the back and into his office.

"Sit down, Jackie, please. Can I get you a tea, coffee, water?"

Jackie sat down.

"You can tell me exactly why a bag full of money is in my garage, Leon. That's what you can do."

Leon sat down at his desk.

"Okay, Jackie. I will tell you, but this is Adam's doing, not mine. I have been inadvertently pulled into this mess."

"Tell me, Leon. Please."

Leon proceeded to tell her the whole story. From the man who initially deposited the bag, to Adam finding the locker key in the overcoat, to the man whose coat it was coming into the shop demanding the bag which Adam had already taken, to finally the visit from the three heavies whose money it was.

He then told her Adam's plan to sit on the money and then use it to pay off all their debts and for Leon to come in on it and split the profits.

Jackie sat there dumbfounded.

She found it hard to believe her husband could do something like this.

"I am shocked beyond belief. Adam wouldn't steal anything. He is such a stickler for things like that."

Leon saw tears well up in her eyes.

"Look, Jackie. Adam was worried about both your financial states, especially with the baby on the way and him with no solid work. This country at present is in a right mess and it doesn't look like it will fix itself anytime soon. Adam tried to put a brave face on things, but he was deeply concerned. This money was a way out for him."

"But it's not his money, Leon. He stole it, for Christ's sake."

Leon held up a pacifying hand.

"I know, Jackie. But it was dirty money. Drugs money, probably. Money that would not be missed. Money that its owner wasn't going to go to the police about. Essentially, it was there for the taking. Rightly or wrongly."

Jackie held her head in her hands.

"What about these men who came here looking for the money? Will they be able to trace it?"

"No, not now. I will keep it here in a locker. They will be back, no doubt. Then, I will paint this all as a misunderstanding and give them it back. I will sort it. I promise," assured Leon.

Jackie nodded and seemed a little more relaxed.

"How much money is in the bag?"

Leon smiled.

"£350,000."

Jackie's mouth hung open.

"My God. What was Adam thinking!"

"I guess he wasn't thinking straight. Go home and talk to him. Sort yourselves out before this baby arrives. It was a moment of madness on his part and mine, to an extent. He was desperate to please you. It was lovely to dream for a minute. But now I need to right things. It will be okay."

Jackie stood and came around the side of the desk and hugged Leon.

"Thank you, Leon. I really mean that."

Leon smiled.

"Hey, that's what friends are for. Now go home."

Leon reached in his pocket and produced his wallet. Opening it, he pulled out two £20 notes."

"Your cab fare. I'll see you both soon, and don't worry. I will take care of everything. And Jackie, don't give him too hard a time. His intentions were good."

Jackie nodded and left.

* * *

The Mercedes pulled up outside Adam's house.

Ronnie spoke.

"Right, is anybody else in the house?"

Adam stared nervously around at the men.

"My wife, maybe?"

Ronnie regarded the house.

"Right, Marcus. Go with him into the house and check it out. We will wait here for the all clear."

Marcus nodded and got out of the car, gesturing for Adam to follow.

Both men walked up to the front door and, with shaking hands, Adam inserted his key in the lock and opened it.

Adam looked at the big, black man.

"My wife is heavily pregnant. Please don't scare her."

Marcus said nothing. He just pushed Adam inside.

Once in the house, Adam went straight to the living room, but it was empty. So was the kitchen. Maybe Jackie was taking a nap.

He headed upstairs with Marcus close behind.

The master bedroom was empty.

A search of the rest of the house confirmed Jackie was not in.

Adam breathed a sigh of relief.

Marcus moved to the open front door and gestured to Ronnie.

Ronnie turned to Ritchie.

"Get in the front here and keep Tommy company in case he gets any ideas of legging it. Hopefully, I won't be long."

Ronnie got out, walked up to the front door and spoke to Adam.

"Right, where is it?"

"In the garage," replied Adam.

"Let's get it then, shall we? Lead the way. And no funny business!"

Ronnie and Marcus followed Adam and watched him open the garage door and slide it up.

The three men entered.

Marcus pulled the door down again as Adam flicked on the lights.

Immediately, he knew something wasn't right. Things had been moved around in here since last time.

He hurried to the work bench and pulled away the boxes and sacking from beside it.

His heart sunk.

The bag was gone.

Adam looked at the empty space where the bag had been and almost willed it to be there.

Ronnie sensed something was wrong.

"What is it?" he asked.

"It's gone," replied Adam.

His voice was a whisper.

"What do you mean 'gone'?" growled Ronnie.

Adam's whole body shook with fear and disbelief.

"It was here in the corner. It's now gone. Somebody has taken it."

"Don't fuck me about, son," shouted Ronnie.

Panic came into Adam's voice.

"It's not fucking there. I am telling the truth."

Before he could continue, Adam felt an electrifying shock go through his body as Marcus thrust the stun gun into his lower back.

He howled in pain and collapsed against the work bench.

"Have some respect, you punk. You are talking to the boss."

Ronnie came forward and lent in close to Adam.

"Who had it?"

Adam got his breath and steadied himself.

"My wife must have found it."

"If that's true, then where would she go with it?"

Ronnie grabbed Adam, span him around and grabbed him by the throat.

"Where?"

"I don't know," croaked Adam.

"Think."

Suddenly, they heard a vehicle pull up outside.

Ronnie's mobile rang and he instantly answered it.

"Yes, Ritchie."

"A taxi has just pulled up, boss, and a woman has got out. She is heading up the garden path to the front door."

Ronnie pocketed his phone and looked at Marcus.

"Looks like the wife is home. Go get her."

Adam struggled.

"No, please don't hurt her. She's pregnant, for God's sake."

Ronnie headbutted Adam full in the face before smartly bringing his knee up into his balls.

Adam sank to the floor and lay helplessly as he saw Marcus open the garage door and disappear outside.

He tried to shout a warning, but he was in too much pain to find his voice.

***

As Jackie inserted her key in the lock and opened the door, Marcus moved up behind her and grabbed her shoulders in a vice like grip.

He whispered in her ear.

"Do as I say if you don't want to get hurt."

Jackie did as she was told.

Minutes later, she stood in the garage looking at her husband lying on the floor.

"What the hell is going on here? Who are you?" she asked.

Ronnie smiled.

"My name is Ronnie Moon and I am the man whose money you took from here. The money your thieving toe rag of a husband stole from me."

As he said this, he drove a sharp kick into Adam's ribs.

Jackie shouted out.

"No. Don't hurt him anymore. Stop and I will tell you where the money is. It is safe. Go get it and, for God's sake, leave us alone."

Ronnie's eyes narrowed.

"Where is it?"

Jackie looked at him with hatred.

"I brought it back to *Luggage Safe* where you initially deposited it. I gave it to the manager, Leon Biggs, and he said he would hold it there until you returned for it."

"Right. Marcus, stay here with this joker while the woman comes with me for insurance. Just in case this is another lie."

Adam tried to rise to protest, but Marcus knelt on his neck.

Ronnie grabbed Jackie by the arm.

"Now, we are going outside and getting in the Merc out there. Don't cause a scene or your husband dies. Do you understand?"

Jackie nodded.

Before she was led away, she stole one last look at her stricken husband.

"What have you done, Adam? How could you risk our lives and the baby's?" she said.

Adam closed his eyes in shame.

She was right. He had been a fool, but he had been seduced by the money and the better life it could have provided for them.

Now, he was in danger of losing everything that was precious to him.

He had seen how ruthless these men could be in pursuit of the money.

He prayed Jackie would be returned safely to him.

Adam couldn't contemplate the alternative.

Chapter 17

Leon had sat at his desk for some time looking at the open bag of money. He had locked the office door after Jackie left and then opened the bag. He had pulled out a bundle and let it flick through his fingers. The touch and the smell made him feel good.

He was glad that the bag had been returned. He hadn't relished another visit from those thugs without the money being here.

After their last visit, he had to do everything in his power to stop Emily and the lad who had been knocked out, Connor, going to the police.

He had spun a story about them being disgruntled customers over a lost bag and if Leon went to the police, they would come back and set fire to the place. They also knew where all the members of staff lived. That and the promise of a bonus in their wages pacified them both for now.

Leon zipped the bag back up and picked it up.

A decision had been made.

He now opened the office door and walked down the corridor to the locker room.

It was empty.

He glanced around the corner and saw there was one member of staff on reception duty.

It was the young Somalian lad, Assad Ismail.

Leon called out to him.

"Assad, take your break now. I'll keep an eye on things."

The young man smiled.

"Thank you, Leon."

As soon as he had gone, Leon walked out the reception door, through *News Plus*, and headed towards the underground carpark across the road where his red Ford Mondeo was parked. In his right hand, he tightly gripped the holdall full of money.

Fuck it. Adam was right. He deserved it. He had worked his balls off since leaving college. But all he had been doing was paying bills and penny pinching.

He was going nowhere in a dead-end job and a dead-end relationship.

Maureen was okay, but she wasn't exactly a Holly Willoughby or a Kelly Brook. With this kind of money, he would have women falling at his feet.

He could live the playboy lifestyle abroad for as long as it lasted.

Fuck it. It had to be better than the existence he was living here.

He would be at that comic con in San Diego.

He would be hitting the tables in Las Vegas.

When he flashed the cash, he would no longer just be the loser comic geek fat boy.

He would finally be somebody.

He would have proper respect.

Bollocks to Adam. The money was his now.

You only live once.

He was out of here and onto a better life.

Those thugs would never find him.

* * *

As the Mercedes pulled up outside Temple Meads Station, Jackie looked out the passenger side window and saw Leon Biggs purposefully striding across the road with the holdall in his hand.

What was he up to? Where was he heading with the money? He told her that he would keep it at Luggage Safe.

That money had to come back to these men in the car or her husband might die.

"There is the manager, Leon," she exclaimed.

Ronnie turned in his seat and looked in the direction Jackie was pointing.

Tommy also looked.

"That's the fat bastard and he has got the holdall. He's fucking having it away."

"The hell he is! Ritchie, get him now!" snarled Ronnie

Tommy intervened.

"Ronnie. Let me get him. I know I've let you down and you're not going to forgive me, but at least this make some amends."

Ronnie regarded him.

"Go on then. But Ritchie will be at a distance behind you."

Tommy smiled and opened the door.

"Here," called Ritchie.

He handed Tommy the Stanley knife.

Tommy took it and slipped it in his jacket pocket.

* * *

Leon now slid behind the wheel of his car and put the bag on the passenger seat.

He planned to go home as he knew Mo was at work. He would quickly pack a case and grab his passport, then he would head over to Brighton. He knew an old college mate he kept in touch with that lived there. Jerry Ingle. He was always asking him to visit.

Leon could go there for a few days and then make plans to get across the channel to France and then disappear into Europe and then further afield. Florida maybe? Hawaii or Las Vegas? Who knew?

Leon Biggs, this is the start of a new and exciting life.

He started the car and began to reverse out of his space in the underground car park.

The place was ominously quiet.

But it was perfect for Leon to make his exit unseen.

Suddenly, the passenger side door was yanked open and Tommy reached in to grab the bag. Leon was startled, but reacted surprisingly quickly for a big man and grabbed the holdall as well.

Both men struggled for control.

The car stalled and Leon had to jam on the handbrake to stop it rolling forward into a concrete pillar.

Leon was stronger than Tommy and was beginning to win the battle, so Tommy produced the Stanley knife and slashed it across the back of the other man's hand laying it open.

Leon squealed in pain and let go of the bag.

Tommy grabbed it.

Leon was not going to lose this money or the opportunities it would bring.

He had made up his mind.

It was no more Mr Nice Guy.

As Tommy walked away with the bag towards the approaching Ritchie, Leon restarted the car, span it around and then gunned it towards the disappearing man.

* * *

Tommy was well pleased. He had redeemed himself in some small way. Maybe things would work out alright after all.

He called out to Ritchie.

"I got it, man. I have fucking got it back."

He then saw the look of surprise and shock on the other man's face and was confused.

Then, he heard the noise of a car.

Tommy had been so wrapped up in his victory, adrenaline had momentarily affected his audio ability.

He now turned around, but it was too late.

The car hit him full on and sent him up and over the bonnet.

Leon stopped and struggled his bulk out of the driver's door.

His hands were slippery with blood from his wound.

He ignored the pain.

He ran over to the unmoving figure on the ground.

Blood was beginning to pool around his head like a crimson halo.

Leon ignored the man and bent down to pick up the bag.

As he gripped it, he felt a huge explosion of pain in his jaw as Ritchie Cummings kicked him full in the face.

Leon fell to all fours stunned.

Ritchie moved in for the kill.

He kicked Leon repeatedly in the ribs and then stomped down on his head viciously.

Ritchie now picked up the bag and then looked down at the hapless man.

Leon rolled over semi-conscious and lay on his back like a beached whale.

"You cheeky, thieving fucker. You're going to pay for this," said Ritchie.

Leon's eyes opened wide in fear as he stared into the barrel of a gun.

His life flashed in front of him.

He squeezed his eyes closed tightly and waited for the bullet.

Leon heard the man say.

"Get up on your feet and go to the car."

Leon got to his feet unsteadily. He was still groggy from the kicks and his jaw felt like it was broken.

Ritchie gestured with the gun for Leon to go to the Mondeo.

He opened the boot.

"Get in, fat boy."

Leon was horrified.

"I can't. I'll never fit. Plus, I'm claustrophobic."

"Get in. Or I'll put a bullet in you where you stand."

Ritchie pushed Leon forward and watched him climb in.

As soon as he was inside, he slammed the boot shut and moved around to the driver's side and jumped in.

He then pulled out his mobile, pressed a number and spoke when it was answered .

"Boss, I have the bag."

"Good work, Ritchie," replied Ronnie Moon.

"I'm in the fat boy's car and he is in the boot. I plan to dispose of the car and its contents on route back to the Cotswolds if that is okay with you."

"Yeah, that's fine by me. That bastard needs a lesson in respect. Where's Tommy?"

"The fat boy ran him down in his car. It doesn't look good. I think he's dead. We need to get out of here, boss."

Ronnie took in Ritchie's words.

How was he going to explain this to Sharon?

He needed to get out of this area and get back home. Once there, he would think about his next move.

For now, he had his money back. That was the most important thing.

"Right, bring me the bag now and I will then drive the woman back home and pick up Marcus. I'll see you back at my house asap."

* * *

Ritchie drove out of the car park and across the road to the Merc.

He would find a secluded spot somewhere to torch the car and fry that fat fucker in the boot.

He had noticed a filled petrol can in the boot when he opened it.

There would be no trace of anything once he had used it.

* * *

Ronnie flipped the boot switch. It opened and Ritchie dropped the bag inside and shut it down again.

"I'll ring you later, Ronnie, when the job is done."

Ronnie nodded.

"Good work."

He heard a siren now getting closer.

A police car and an ambulance swung around the corner towards the car park.

Ritchie passed them going the other way .

Ronnie watched him disappear from sight.

He regarded Jackie in the passenger seat.

"I'm taking you back home now."

Jackie nodded.

"My husband, what are you going to do to him?"

"He's been a naughty boy. He stole from me. I can't let that go unpunished. He needs to have a reminder of the error of his ways so that he will remember for the rest of his life."

"Please don't hurt him. Our baby is due soon. He made a really bad mistake. He knows that now. You have your money. Please just go and leave us be."

"It doesn't work like that. If I let him off the hook and the word goes around, every chancer will think he can steal from me. It's the law of the jungle. He pays."

Jackie went to speak, but Ronnie cut her off.

"Enough. Be quiet now. Your pleas are falling on deaf ears. Now, don't push me anymore."

Jackie looked at Ronnie through teary eyes.

"I fucking hate you. I hate you."

Ronnie backhanded Jackie hard across the face, splitting her lip.

"I said shut up and I meant it."

Jackie cowered in the passenger seat quietly sobbing.

As Ronnie waited to pull out into the traffic, Jackie realised that, in all the commotion, he had forgotten to lock the car doors after opening the boot.

She waited until he was checking over his shoulder for a gap to drive off and then she pulled the handle and got out the car as quickly as she could.

Ronnie reacted too late and she headed across the road to the underground car park and the police.

He cursed under his breath.

Fuck it, he would have to let her go.

He pulled away from the kerb heading back to the house.

He rang Marcus to let him know he was coming.

"Marcus, I'm on my way back. I have the money, but the woman has done a runner. I suspect she is going to inform the police and they will be on their way there soon. Sort the man out with a little reminder of his error and then get out of there. Keep me in phone contact and I will pick you up somewhere in the area. Okay?"

"Will do, boss," replied Marcus.

* * *

Marcus pocketed his phone and looked at Adam who was lying on the floor of the garage by the work bench.

The big man moved towards him.

"You will be pleased to know I will be leaving soon and your wife is okay. But before I go, the boss told me to give you a little present."

With that said, he produced the stun gun from his coat and closed in on Adam.

Adam shuffled and cowered into the corner. Marcus pushed the stun gun against his ribs and pressed it. A crack of electricity coursed through Adam's body, making his teeth shake in his gums.

Adam cried in pain and rolled into a ball.

Marcus pressed it again into his thigh.

Adam spasmed like a puppet on a string.

Through tears of pain, he cried out.

"No more, please. For God's sake."

Marcus smiled ruthlessly .

"It's not quite over yet, boy. Now I am going to mark you. So when you look in the mirror every day when you shave, you will have a reminder of what you've done."

With that, he reached into his trouser pocket and produced a vicious-looking knife. It had a curved four-inch blade and glinted ominously under the glow of the fluorescent light.

Marcus also produced his phone.

"I need to film this bit so the boss can see that I have done the job properly."

Fear like he never knew gripped Adam's very soul.

He frantically reached back under the work bench where he knew his toolbox was.

The lid was open.

He reached in and his hand wrapped around what he was after.

Marcus reached down and grabbed Adam by the hair.

"Now, hold still. I don't want to cut your throat. Just your face."

As Marcus moved the knife closer, Adam pulled his hand out of the toolbox, brandishing a thin wood chisel.

He plunged it hard and fast high up to the inside of the big man's thigh.

By luck more than judgment, the chisel severed the femoral artery by the groin and blood erupted from it like a geyser.

Marcus froze in pain, watching the blood spurt from his wound. He dropped his knife and phone to the floor, now using both hands to try and stem the flow of blood.

Fear filled the big man's eyes.

A fatal major artery had been severed. He needed to stem the blood flow fast with some sort of tourniquet.

Adam saw his chance and staggered to his feet.

At the same time, he picked up the discarded knife and pocketed the phone.

He thought he could hear sirens approaching, but wasn't sure if it was his imagination.

As Marcus staggered back against the work bench, Adam ran forward and drove the blade into the side of the big man's neck.

He watched as Marcus's eyes bulged in shock and pain.

He now clawed frantically at his neck before collapsing to the floor.

Adam moved to the garage door and opened it. Daylight streamed in which blinded him.

He ran outside nearly colliding into his wife, Jackie, and two police officers.

Jackie hugged him tightly as they both sobbed.

The police and paramedics moved towards the garage.

***

Ronnie pulled up at the end of Adam and Jackie's street.

From his car, he saw an armed response vehicle pulling away from the house. Two police patrol cars and an ambulance were parked up outside.

He could see both Adam and Jackie sat on the garden wall talking to a plain clothes policeman.

There was no sign of Marcus, which didn't bode well.

Ronnie had to get out of there and back home away from this chaos.

What a mess this had turned out to be, but he did have the money.

A black van now pulled up outside.

It was a crime scene investigation vehicle.

This was not good news.

What in God's name had happened?

He pulled away and left the scene as quickly as possible, anxious to make distance between himself and the crime scene.

He got onto the M32, which would eventually connect him to the M5.

He turned on the radio and almost instantly a news flash interrupted Don McLean singing 'American Pie'.

The news informed him about a hit and run accident in an underground carpark by Bristol Temple Meads Train Station.

One man was knocked over by a mystery driver.

The victim was rushed to Southmead Hospital, where his condition was described as critical but stable.

Fuck, Tommy was alive after all.

Another piece of breaking news reported the death of a man in Fishponds.

Early indications were that the man was robbing the house, but the owners put up a fight and the robber was killed.

Shit, Marcus was dead. That little thieving shit killed him, but how? Marcus was solid. A pro. What had gone wrong?

As the Mercedes joined the M5 heading for Gloucestershire, Ronnie rang Sharon using the hands-free Bluetooth.

She answered almost immediately.

"Ronnie, what's going on? How's Tommy? Did you find him?"

"Listen up, Sharon. I have the money back, but Tommy got knocked over in a hit and run. I had nothing to do with it. I will fill you in on the details later. For now, the news says he is stable and is at Southmead Hospital. Go and see him."

"Christ, Ronnie. If he dies, I will never forgive you," sobbed Sharon.

"I told you, I never touched him."

"Yes, but he is where he's at because of you."

Ronnie laughed.

"Is that so? Well, let me remind you that it was you who begged me to give him a job and when I did, he fucked it up. This whole situation has originated from that asshole of a husband of yours and don't you forget it. So, I think the both of you have to shoulder the blame for the outcome. Let's face it. It was never going to be good. I only came looking for what was mine."

"You bastard, Ronnie! That may be so, but wherever you go, you bring trouble and danger. You could have given him a legitimate job in one of your businesses, not something dodgy."

"Yes, I could have. But what is Tommy qualified to do, apart from pissing it up and smoking weed? He hasn't exactly got a full and interesting CV, has he? He is a waste of space, so he wasn't in a position to pick and choose a job. If he had been, he would have gone out and got one without my help."

Although the words deeply wounded her, she knew what Ronnie had said was true to some extent, but she was angry and also worried for Tommy's health.

"I'm going to the hospital now. This conversation is over. I want you to stay away from me and never contact me again. Do you understand?"

Ronnie was silent for a moment before he replied.

"Are you sure, Sharon? Have a good think before you burn all your bridges. What if Tommy doesn't pull through or he is severely handicapped? You will need support. You will need money."

Sharon's anger and pride would not allow her to change her opinion.

"I will have to cope. But I will do it without you. You are bad news, Ronnie. You always have been."

"Okay, Sharon. You have made yourself perfectly clear. Have a good life and oh, give my regards to Tommy if he regains consciousness."

He hung up before she could reply.

What was done was done.

Time to move on.

Chapter 18

The road had been cordoned off and the garage was being treated as a murder scene.

After a brief talk with the police, Adam was taken off in the ambulance for a thorough check over at hospital. He was in a state of shock. Jackie was also brought with him to be examined to make sure the baby was okay and not in distress.

The police said they would see them tomorrow for a more formal interview.

This was good for Jackie as she needed to think about Adam's and her stories and make sure they tied up. In no way must they know that Adam stole the bag of money.

The only other person who knew was Leon, but he never reappeared from the underground car park and that thug returning the bag to Ronnie Moon had suggested something unpleasant had happened to him.

She didn't want to think about it.

From the brief talk she had with the police straight after the incident, she told them that two men had randomly knocked on their door and when Adam answered, they pushed their way into their home and asked for money. When they told them they had no cash in the house, Adam was tortured with a stun gun, but to no avail.

Eventually, one of the men took Jackie in a car to an ATM machine to get her to make a withdrawal. The other man had stayed with Adam to make sure his wife did as she was told.

Adam, who had been in shock, could not coherently explain what had happened in the garage.

Jackie obviously had no knowledge of what had taken place.

That interview would have to wait until Adam was clearer on the facts.

The police had then asked Jackie how she had ended up so far away from her home at Temple Meads looking for an ATM machine when there were two in her neighbourhood.

Thinking fast on her feet, Jackie had replied that the machines closer to home all had queues outside them so they had gone looking for a more secluded one.

She also played dumb when asked about the make or model of the car she was driven in, telling them that she had no idea about cars, only that this one was big and silver in colour.

The police also asked if she could identify the man who drove the car. She said yes, but she knew that she could paint any picture of this man she wanted as long as Adam said the same.

She went on to tell them that some sort of incident had occurred outside the station, which brought the police to the scene. This had prompted her to escape the car and head for them.

The police for now had seemed satisfied with her story.

She just needed the time to brief Adam about it when he was well enough before the formal interview.

From the police's point of view, her story sounded feasible.

It strangely tied up with another recent call the police had received from a Lisa Miller, informing them that she had encountered some strange men in her neighbour's house when she knocked on the door a few nights ago.

They seemed suspicious and she hadn't seen them there before.

When the police had arrived and entered the house after no answer, there was nobody inside.

At present, they were looking for the house owner, a Mr Finlay Bryant, who was apparently missing.

Jackie had concocted her part of the story to make sure Adam was not incriminated in any way.

The man who had taken the money had got what he wanted.

She didn't see him coming back any time soon.

Much too risky.

Adam and she were in the clear.

She would have the baby and they would be one happy family together.

They would be alright. They would find a way.

She prayed Adam would get over the terrible trauma of what had happened in the garage.

Jackie hoped the new baby and time would heal him.

They would learn to deal with the situation. For now, the main thing was they were in the clear.

* * *

Jackie was given a clean bill of health. The baby was fine and everything was as it should be. She now waited to hear about Adam. It would be a while yet before she could see him, but the prognosis was good.

As she waited, she slipped out into the hospital grounds.

Jackie now took out the mobile phone she had found in Adam's jacket pocket when they had removed it to initially examine his wounds in the ambulance.

She had been handed the jacket and that's when she had found the strange phone.

All his clothes were to be held for a forensic examination, but she had managed to take the phone without anybody noticing.

Now, in the garden, she looked at it.

It was a simple pay-as-you-go burner.

There was only one phone number listed in it and she guessed it was the man who had taken her off in the Mercedes.

The man whose money Adam had taken.

She drew a deep breath and pushed the number.

Her hands were trembling.

* * *

Ronnie had just spoken to Ritchie. He had informed him that he had torched the car and its passenger.

On the way to the location, he called Harry Giles, another trusted member of the firm, to come and pick him up.

He was now about twenty minutes from Ronnie's house.

Ronnie told him he was about half an hour away and would meet him there.

He also let Ritchie know that he was almost sure they had lost Marcus.

Ritchie remained silent.

Ronnie went on to tell him that, when they met up, they would discuss their story and whereabouts the last few days just in case the police might come sniffing.

He was ninety-nine percent sure they were in the clear, but he hadn't got to where he was in life without being thorough and covering his tracks.

As he ended the call, the phone rang again.

Strange, as only Ritchie and Marcus had access to this burner phone number.

Could Marcus be alive?

He cautiously pressed the button.

"Yeah?"

"Mr Moon, this is Jackie Lucas here."

Ronnie chuckled to himself.

"You have got some neck, sweetheart. I give you that. I underestimated you and your old man. What can I do for you?"

"Your man is dead. He died in a struggle with Adam. The police are all over the scene. So far, I haven't mentioned your name at all. My husband made a big mistake stealing your money, but you now have it back and nobody is any the wiser. You are in the clear."

She paused.

"Go on. I am listening," said Ronnie.

"I have spun the story that two random men forced their way into our house demanding cash and when we didn't have any to hand, I was driven to an ATM while one of the men watched over my husband. The real reason is buried and I don't see any reason to bring it up.

The only other person involved with the stolen money was the manager of *Luggage Safe,* a Leon Biggs, but I guess your other thug has long taken care of him?"

Ronnie remained silent.

"Anyway, I can give any description that I want to the police in connection to the man who drove me to the cash machine. I can also forget the make, model and registration plate of the vehicle or not, depending on you."

Ronnie shook his head in amazement. This pregnant little housewife had suddenly turned into GI Jane with an attitude.

"So, what do you want from me?"

Jackie took another deep breath.

"For you to take your money and go home and leave me and my family alone. Enough people have suffered over this."

"Don't forget, lady. Your husband has a lot to do with that," replied Ronnie.

"I know. But at the end of the day, he is my husband and I will stand by him no matter what."

For a fleeting moment thought, Ronnie thought of Sharon and Tommy.

Sharon had fought him tooth and nail all the way over her husband, even though he had fucked up. He had to admire both women.

"That's it?" he asked.

"Yes, that's it."

"Alright, you have my word. It's over," said Ronnie.

"Okay. Then that's it. I make a story up for the police and you are in the clear and so is Adam," replied Jackie.

"You are a smart cookie, darling. That old man of yours is lucky you are in his corner. You have my word. It is over and done."

Jackie felt tears welling up in her eyes.

"Thank you," she whispered.

The phone went dead.

She sat down on a wooden bench and composed herself.

Jackie pocketed the phone.

She would keep it just in case. She also had the registration of the Mercedes locked down in her own phone as insurance.

Her dad had been a used car salesman. She knew her makes and models of cars very well.

***

When she entered the ward again, Adam was settled comfortably in bed. He was alone. He smiled when he saw her come in.

They hugged.

"Are you okay?" Jackie asked.

"I think so, yes. A little sore, but I'll live. Is it over?"

Jackie smiled and nodded.

"Yes, it's over and we're safe."

Tears now formed in Adam's eyes.

"I'm so sorry for what I did and putting you and the baby in danger. That was never my intention. I love you so much. I would never hurt you. I was a fool. I..."

Jackie put a finger to his lips.

"Let's not talk about that now. That can wait until another day. Right now, there are a few things I need to straighten out with you before the police interview us again."

She knew things would be alright.

The baby being born would be extra expense so the £10,000 she had kept back from the bag and hidden inside the big blue teddy in the nursery room of their house would come in handy down the line.

Chapter 19

Ronnie came down over the hill and saw the familiar lights from the houses of Stonebridge village at the bottom.

He was tired and the hour was late.

The whole incident had been a bit hit and miss and the loss of Marcus was a blow, but he had the money, which was the main thing.

He thought of Tommy. That bastard had more lives than a cat. He suspected he would pull through, which he was pleased about for Sharon's sake.

Even after their recent conversation, she was still his sister and he would always keep an eye on her, even if it had to be from afar.

Mostly, he was pissed off that he had to leave the Cotswolds and slip back into his other persona of Ronnie Moon, gangster and criminal.

He hated it when some insignificant, little toerag forced him to go hands on again. Ronnie was getting too old for the violence. He had others on his payroll to do that stuff. He wanted to distance himself from it.

Living in the sleepy village of Stonebridge with Josie was good. The relaxed atmosphere did wonders for his ulcer and blood pressure.

Thinking of Josie, he gave her a call, but it went to answerphone.

Probably in the bath or maybe had an early night?

It would be good to see her and give her a cuddle and tell her everything was alright.

The welcoming lights got closer and, soon, Ronnie was cruising through the market square and heading for Foxglove Lane that would lead to his property.

* * *

As Ronnie pulled the Mercedes up to the gates of his property, he pressed a remote control, which opened them and allowed him to drive on in. He followed the gravel road around to the large sweeping driveway and forecourt.

There were no other parked cars, except Josie's MG convertible.

Ritchie had been dropped off and was probably inside helping himself to Ronnie's best malt.

Ronnie smiled.

Fuck it. He deserved it. He had done a good job and retrieved the money.

As Ronnie got out of his car, he mused that he could murder a scotch as well.

After getting the bag from the boot, he walked up the steps to the front door.

The house was in darkness, except for one light burning downstairs somewhere.

For some reason, Ronnie suddenly felt a feeling of unease.

He looked around him at the bushes and trees and noticed the many pockets of shadows they gave. For a few moments, he was transported back to the shooting.

It had been quiet and dark just like this that night.

He pulled out his door keys and let himself in.

The hallway was in darkness.

Unusual as Josie usually leaves a lamp on when she goes to bed.

Ronnie dropped his bag, took off his jacket and hung it up on a peg. He also took off his gun holster and hung that up as well. He would put it in the safe in the morning.

All he wanted now was a scotch, a warm shower and then crawl into bed next to his wife.

He went into the living room to get his drink.

The light he had seen from outside was from the television and, to his relief, he saw Ritchie led out on the sofa.

As suspected, an empty crystal glass tumbler sat on the coffee table.

He was sleeping.

Ronnie walked over to the coffee table, picked up the remote and flipped the television off.

He regarded Ritchie.

Pushing his shoulder, Ronnie said, "Wake up, sleeping beauty. I'm home."

Ritchie didn't move.

Ronnie pushed him once more, this time harder.

"I said, wake up, you lazy bastard."

There was no movement.

A sense of unease washed over Ronnie yet again.

He switched on the table lamp and then recoiled in horror.

Ritchie's throat had been slit clean open.

Ronnie backed away and then span around, surveying the room.

He then thought.

Josie.

He ran back out into the hallway, crossed to where his coat hung and took the handgun out of its holster.

The house was deafly silent, except for the ticking of the wall clock.

He didn't know whether to reveal himself or not, but he couldn't waste time searching every room for Josie.

He had to know she was alive.

"Josie? Josie? Are you alright? Answer me."

He then heard her voice sounding from the kitchen.

"I'm in the kitchen. Hurry Ronnie, please."

She sounded scared, but alive.

Thank God.

* * *

Ronnie cautiously pushed open the kitchen door and walked in, gun pointing forward.

The sight he saw made him freeze momentarily.

Josie was sat on a stool at the kitchen island.

Her hands were bound.

Beside her stood a mountain of a man. His bald head and bushy beard reminded Ronnie of the singer Rag and Bone Man.

The guy held an ominous looking black Glock 17 to her head. Another man also stood in the kitchen and his gun was trained on Ronnie.

He was smartly dressed in an expensive black designer suit. His salt and pepper hair was cut stylishly and his goatee beard was trimmed to perfection.

"Drop the gun now, Mr Moon," he instructed.

His accent was Russian.

Ronnie regarded the two men and every fibre of his being wanted to start shooting.

The man seemed to sense this.

"Don't be foolish; otherwise, your lovely wife will die."

To emphasise this, the man mountain pulled Josie tighter towards him.

Ronnie dropped the gun.

The man smiled.

"Good."

"Who the fuck are you and what do you want?" asked Ronnie.

The man smiled.

"That is what your friend in the living room said before he died. Unfortunately, we had to kill your dog as well because it didn't seem to like us. But yes, how rude of me. The man with your wife is Dmitriy. My name is Nikolay Petrov. You don't know me, but you have met my little brother Pavel. You killed him."

It was Ronnie's turn to smile.

"Ah right, you mean the little shit who shot me. The gutless bastard deserved what he got. He had his chance and blew it. I didn't. As they say, all is fair in love and war."

"Yes, my brother did mess up, but he was still my brother and you took his life along with some of my other colleagues. That has to be answered."

Ronnie's features hardened.

"Your boss made the mistake of trying to muscle in on my patch. Did you think I was just going to sit back and let you jokers waltz in? Come on. You know the score. Live by the sword and die by the sword. It's the nature of the business we are in."

"True," replied Nikolay, "But this is not to do with business. This is family. Blood. Do you know what it feels like to have somebody you love taken away from you?"

Ronnie was silent. He didn't like the way this conservation was going.

"No. I doubt you do, so let me show you, Mr Moon."

Before Ronnie could respond, the man mountain pulled the trigger of the Glock.

Josie was dead before her body collapsed to the kitchen floor.

Time seemed to stand still.

Then an ear-piercing roar echoed around the kitchen.

"Noooooooooo!"

It was Ronnie.

He looked at his beautiful wife.

Half her head was missing and blood and brains covered the breakfast bar.

Ronnie roared again and ran at the man called Nikolay.

Nikolay was momentarily surprised by the speed that Ronnie moved, but he managed to get a shot off that smashed into Ronnie's shoulder before he was hit by a tackle that took his breath away.

Ronnie drove the man back with incredible force, borne out of hatred and despair.

Both men crashed straight through the patio windows in a shower of glass and landed on the concrete.

Ronnie ignored his pain and straddled Nikolay's chest, raining down punches into the man's face, breaking his nose and opening cuts over and under his eyes.

His hatred knew no bounds.

He now smashed his head down over and over into the man before sinking his teeth deeply into the side of his neck and shook and tore at the flesh like a rabid dog looking to rip out the carotid artery and jugular vein.

Suddenly, he felt himself being pulled away.

Dmitriy hauled him clear like a rag doll.

Ronnie got to his knees.

His eyes were glazed and bright red blood stained his mouth.

"Fuck you, asshole," he hissed.

He then smiled crazily and ran forward.

Dmitriy levelled his gun and fired.

A bullet hit Ronnie square in the chest sending him flying back into the wall.

Another hit him in the same spot and he slid down the wall to the floor.

The big man moved forward and levelled the gun at Ronnie's head.

Ronnie smiled ruefully and spat a mouthful of blood at him.

"Go on then, wanker. Do it. Get it over with. By the way, I hope Ukraine fuck your country up!"

Dmitriy pulled the trigger and Ronnie died instantly.

The big man moved over to where his colleague lay.

He was in a bad way. Barely conscious. But both men's eyes met and Nikolay nodded.

Dmitriy put a bullet in his head before leaving the premises over the back wall the way they had come in.

Chapter 20

Eddie Sweeney pulled his 4x4 Jeep up outside Ronnie Moon's house. He had been surprised to find the gates open at the driveway entrance. Normally, he would have to press the wall intercom for access.

He had a 7.00am PT session with the lovely Josie.

Sweet work when you can get it.

He reckoned she fancied him, but he wasn't going to go there.

For one thing, her husband was a scary bastard. More to him than met the eye.

From Eddie's background in the forces, he knew a tough motherfucker when he met one.

Secondly, he needed their money as he was in the middle of going through a messy divorce.

His wife, Sheila, was screwing him for every penny possible. Plus, she was having custody of their kids, Ruby and Josh. He just could about afford to run his beloved vehicle.

Where the divorce was concerned, Eddie didn't have a leg to stand on. Sheila had come home early one day and found him in their bed with a 'client' from the gym. They were not having the sort of workout Sheila expected. Also, it wasn't the first time she had caught her husband in flagrante. This time, there was no way back for Eddie and she kicked him out.

He was now up to his eyes in debt and living in a shabby one-bedroom room above a public house in a decidedly downbeat part of Cirencester, some ten miles away from the Moons' residence.

Eddie was working all the hours God sent and the money from the Moons was like gold dust at present. So, he wasn't going to fuck it up by doing something stupid.

Sweeney jumped out of his vehicle and looked up at a watery sun breaking through the clouds. The morning was dry and crisp. Maybe a little run around the grounds first with the lady of the house before a gym session.

This gig, which he had now been on for six months, was the best earner he had in a long while since he trained a wannabe celebrity, Danny Howe, for an audition for *Love Island*. As far as Eddie knew, he got a part in the show, but he didn't watch shite like that.

He made his way to the front door and rang the bell.

He waited, but nothing.

Eddie rang three more times, but with no success.

He did have a front door key, but would only ever use it in an emergency .

He now rang both Josie's and Eddie's mobile phones, but both went to answerphone.

This was strange, so reluctantly, he used his key to open the front door.

From the step, he called out their names, but all was silent.

Usually, Harley their dog would have come out to see who it was.

But nothing.

He went to the foot of the stairs and shouted out. Nothing.

Eddie now smelt a faint odour in the air.

It resembled rotten meat.

Heading to the kitchen, he pushed open the door and was taken aback by the carnage that greeted him.

He had seen some shit in a warzone, but this was like a slaughterhouse here in the leafy Cotswolds.

His eyes took in the scene.

Blood was sprayed everywhere.

Ruby red against the stark white background of the floor and kitchen units.

First, Josie sat against the island, most of her face missing.

Eddie turned his eyes away.

He now walked over to the shattered patio doors, careful not to tread in any blood.

A body of a man he did not recognise lay on its back bloodied around the neck with a bullet hole through the forehead.

Then, he saw Ronnie.

His bullet-riddled body lay still with sightless eyes seemingly watching him.

Bloodied footprints traced a path out of the kitchen and down the garden path.

Somebody else had been involved and had done a runner.

What the hell had happened here? A botched burglary? Some dodgy deal gone tits up?

Whatever had happened, they were all dead.

Eddie now wondered if there had been anybody else in the house.

He stealthily checked upstairs. It was clean.

On entering the living room, he found the corpse of the dog behind the door and a corpse of a man he had seen once or twice at the house. A bit of a brute by the looks of him.

Something serious had gone down here last night and Eddie knew he didn't want any part of it.

Shit, he had enough on his plate with the divorce.

Then, rather callously, he suddenly thought, *'There goes my cash cow. Both my best clients dead.'*

Life can be a bitch.

He decided it was time to leave.

A cleaner normally arrived at 9.00am. She was a nosey old bitch named Rose. She could deal with this. She would be dining out on this story for fucking years.

Eddie hurried out into the hallway and towards the front door.

That's when he saw the holdall.

It looked out of place, as if somebody had just dropped it down there in a hurry.

He was drawn to it and curiosity made him open it.

A low whistle came from Eddie as he feasted his eyes on the bundles of used notes.

Shit. He had hit the jackpot.

Maybe this was what it had all been about?

But if that was the case, why leave it behind?

Whatever the reason, Eddie knew this would solve all his money problems and there was nobody around to say otherwise.

When the police eventually arrived, they would confiscate the money and it would probably end up in an incinerator.

Fuck that.

Eddie Sweeney was going to make good use of it.

He zipped up the bag and left the house closing the door quietly behind him.

Popping the backdoor of his 4x4, he deposited the bag in there safely and then got in the driver's seat, sporting a huge grin on his face as he drove down the driveway and out onto the road.

Every cloud and all that!

Within minutes, he was on the main A427 heading back to Cirencester to check out of his room and start a new chapter in his life.

Who said money was the root of all evil.

If you enjoyed this book, then you have to
check out other stories by Kevin.
Read a little about them on the following pages.
Available at Amazon, Waterstones and
all good bookstores.
Join the group Kevin O'Hagan's Author's
Corner on Facebook.
www.kevinohagan.com.

Battlescars

Tony Slade novel no. 1

Some wounds run deep. Can they ever heal?

Tony Slade sits in a coffee shop waiting. He is reflecting on his dark and violent past. He is waiting for the woman he loves, but he is also waiting for the man who wants him dead. Who will reach him first? The clock is ticking...

Tony Slade is used to dealing with violence and death. He has made a career out of it. From boxer to bouncer, paratrooper, and mercenary to minder. But now, he is getting older and he wants out. He has miraculously found love and he has one last chance at happiness, but it will come with a price. The woman he loves is not his; she belongs to a very dangerous man. A man that you don't want to cross. But Tony is ready to risk it all on one last roll of the dice before a powder keg of violence explodes.

But that is not all. Unknown to him, there is another threat coming his way. One that he will not see until the last moment. Who will get out alive?

Tough times call for tough people. Tony Slade is one such person.

No Hiding Place

Tony Slade novel no. 2

You can run but you can't hide forever

They say time is a great healer, but for Tony Slade time is running out. The physical scars are healing, but the mental one's are still raw.

Waking up in hospital after the coffee shop massacre and finding he has cheated death, he needs to know why.

But he has now become a man everybody wants to question.

All he wants to do is disappear forever, but some people will not let that happen.

Suddenly, Tony is hounded by the press and media. He is also trailed by the tenacious DCI Wyatt and he is hunted by a psychotic killer who is relentless and hell bent on revenge.

Tony Slade is in hiding recovering from the bullet wounds and the trauma of recent events that have changed his life forever.

Hiding on the tiny, isolated island of *Graig O Mor* in the Bristol Channel, he knows it is only a matter of time until he is found.

Then he will have to stop running and make a stand against an enemy who will not give up. It will become a matter of life and death.

A storm is coming from the mainland
to the Island of Graig O Mor

Last Stand

Tony Slade novel no. 3

Blood is thicker than water

Tony Slade is living in the Canary Islands. He is resting and soaking up the sun. He is keeping his head down under an assumed identity and trying to forget the last few traumatic years where he has experienced love, violence, heartbreak and death.

Tony is a survivor. An ex-paratrooper and mercenary who has seen more than his fair share of action, but those days are well behind him now. Or so he thought.

He is no longer a young man and the fire that used to burn like an inferno in his belly is now just flickering. Tony is looking for a quiet life into retirement when he receives a shocking and lifechanging piece of news. A secret that has been buried for years has suddenly came to light.

This secret will force Tony out of hiding to return to the UK and back into the violent world of gangsters, drugs and crime.

Pursued all the time by an old nemesis, Tony must pull all his fighting skills together to face a dangerous and deadly drug lord who has something of his that he wants back at any cost. Tony knows that blood will spill in one final stand.

This time it's personal

Killing Time

The clock is ticking, and time is running out

Ex-Scotland Yard policeman DCI Joe Regan had retired from the force after a particularly vicious attempt on his life that had him on the critical list in hospital, but his gritty Gaelic spirit and resolve helped him recover.

Now leading a new life running an Antiques Emporium in the sleepy town of Oakcombe in the West Country, he is trying to put his past behind him.

But unknown to Joe, a burglary at the nearby country home of famous TV celebrity Ron Goodwin opens up a nasty can of worms in the form of something hidden within an antique clock which finds its way to his shop.

This something could ruin Ron Goodwin's career just as he is about to crack America.

The dark secrets contained within the clock cannot afford to fall into the wrong hands, so it must be found at all costs, even if it means murder.

Joe Regan suddenly finds himself embroiled in a race to find the clock as it goes missing and its contents before a hired killer who will stop at nothing does.

But when Joe inadvertently stumbles across the secret, he now becomes the next target.

A Change of Heart

*Can a heart transplant victim inherit
the characteristics of their donor?*

Simon Winter is a prime candidate for a heart attack. Middle aged, sedentary and grossly overweight, his lifestyle is driving him to an early grave, but he is ignoring all the signs until it is too late.

He has a failed marriage behind him, a boring job and a fear of violence and blood. He has lived a safe and uneventful life avoiding confrontation and danger until now where this is all about to change dramatically.

Eddie Prince is an ex-professional boxer and minor television celebrity. He has had a turbulent life out of the ring, which has resulted in prison time. Money has come and gone as he has a gambling addiction, which results in him owing a lot of money to some bad people. He has run away to what he hopes is a better life, but his old life is about to catch up with him, resulting in dire circumstances.

These two men are about to connect in a way they could never have dreamed of. Two men at different ends of the spectrum. Two men who are chalk and cheese. Two men who have nothing in common until one inherits the other's heart after a transplant.

Now, one will use the other as a vessel of revenge to find the man who murdered him and settle a score with shocking conclusions.

Blood Tracks

Stormtrooper were at one time in the 1980s the most successful rock band on the planet. Everything they touched turned to gold. But amongst all the fame was jealousy and greed. This resulted in the sacking of their iconic lead singer, Jimmy Parrish, for drug usage that endangered the band's continued success.

Sometime later after a bitter break-up, Jimmy Parrish apparently committed suicide under mysterious circumstances. His body was never found. A proposed 'warts and all' book on the band that he had been approached to write would now never happen, a blessing for some.

The Mark 2 line-up of the band went on to have global success in the 1980s and entered the Rock and Roll Hall of Fame as one of the biggest rock bands of all time. Even when they finally split up, the spectre of Jimmy Parrish never fully went away.

Fast forward twenty years, the band have reformed to record a new album.

They are heading for the remote island of Ruma off the Outer Hebrides.

Ruma is a wild isolated place of mystery and intrigue.

They will stay at the grand house of a reclusive film director who has a state-of-the-art recording studio in the bowels of the building.

Storm Alec is due to hit the island. It will cut the island and its inhabitants off from the rest of civilisation.

But worse is to come as a mysterious killer lurks within the walls of the house hellbent on murdering each and every member of the band and their recording crew.

Who is it and what is their motive?

There is nowhere to run and nowhere to hide.

Nobody is coming to help.

As the body count rises, who if anybody can survive?

Making a hit record can sometimes be murder.